PRAISE ᴦᴏʀ ⋅ ⋅ ⋅⋅ ⋅ ⋅ ⋅ ⋅ ⋅ ⋅⋅

'I was mesmerised by this superbly written tale and in particular the use of the voice of the narrator. What was even more surprising was the end… Five stars [are] not enough!'

Margaret D, Netgalley reviewer

'The clever twists that come towards the end of the book totally blew me away it was a shocker and made this a most addictive and brilliant read.'

Kat G, Netgalley reviewer

'I really felt like I was there with Catherine trapped in the back of a Transit van with a crying baby which fuels the gang members' anger. The best thing about this novel is the twist in the tale at the end. Unputdownable!!!!'

Sharon A, Netgalley reviewer

'An outstanding, detailed depiction of a hostage situation that makes you feel as if you are there on the scene.'

Janice L, Netgalley reviewer

'I was captivated right away!'

Maryline D, Netgalley reviewer

Nick Louth is a bestselling thriller writer, award-winning financial journalist and an investment commentator. A 1979 graduate of the London School of Economics, he went on to become a Reuters foreign correspondent in 1987. It was an experience at a medical conference in Amsterdam in 1992, while working for Reuters, that gave him the inspiration for *Bite*, which was self-published in 2007 and went on to become the UK no. 1 Kindle bestseller for several weeks in 2014 before being snapped up by Sphere. It has sold a third of a million copies, and been translated into six languages.

The terrorism thriller *Heartbreaker* was published in June 2014 and received critical acclaim from Amazon readers, with a 4.6 out of 5 stars on over 100 reviews. *Mirror Mirror*, subtitled 'When evil and beauty collide', was published in June 2016. *The Body in the Marsh*, a crime thriller, was published by Canelo in September 2017, with *The Body on the Shore* following in 2018.

Freelance since 1998, he has been a regular contributor to the *Financial Times*, *Investors Chronicle* and *Money Observer*, and has published nine other books. Nick Louth is married and lives in Lincolnshire.

www.nicklouth.com

Paperback edition first published in Great Britain in 2019
by Ludensian Books

www.ludensianbooks.co.uk
www.nicklouth.com

eBook first published in Great Britain in 2019 by Canelo

Paperback ISBN: 978-0-85719-750-4
eBook ISBN: 9781788632492

British Library Cataloguing in Publication Data
A CIP catalogue record for this book can be obtained
from the British Library

Trapped

NICK LOUTH

LUDENSIAN BOOKS

For Louise, as always

'The dead don't die. They look on and help.'
D. H. Lawrence

Chapter One

This is my wife, Catherine, yesterday evening. Tuesday. You can see her, with a screwdriver, in the boot of our Nissan, trying to tighten the screws on the anchor points for the new child seat. I tell her that they are secure, the man at the shop who installed it told us so, and he is fully qualified. I'd already double-checked the seat too. Watched the video, read the instructions. Used all my strength to test the straps, wobbled it, tried to pull it loose. It was fine. But for her that wasn't enough. When it comes to Ethan, nothing is ever enough. She fears that in a collision our one-year-old son could be catapulted from the back seat through the windscreen. Since Ethan arrived, Catherine has developed a tendency to worry about all sorts of things. Sometimes it is reasonable, sometimes not.

She is understandably anxious about the odd-shaped mole on her right shoulder. She frets about her figure, and the smile lines she has acquired at 41, and seems to be convinced that one day I will no longer find her attractive. She's wrong. I will adore her to my dying day, I can guarantee that now. I love her corkscrew copper hair and her pale freckled skin, even though she hates it and wishes she were a dark-haired olive-skinned Italian.

Wishing you were something else, someone else, somewhere else. It's so clear to me now that you have what you have, and you make of it what you can. That's what matters. When the time comes, when you are tested. You never know when that will be. I didn't know, and neither here does she, still working on that seat for our son. Look at her. She has no idea of what is going to happen in less than 24 hours. That would make her worry, no mistake.

That mole. Catherine survived skin cancer, you see. She knew about the risks. She never sunbathed, was rarely drawn to the beach, always wore a broad-brimmed hat and gallons of sunscreen when on our brief foreign holidays. She had been aware since childhood that with her milky skin and about as many freckles as a galaxy has stars that there would always be a chance of some malevolent sun-seared alien cell, splitting and growing in a forgotten corner of her epidermis. And she had always looked out for the arrival of that malignity. Believe me, she looked. I saw her after every shower, in front of the mirror. But it was a dab of pigment she noticed for the first time under the nail of her left little toe, just a smear of brown visible through the cuticle, when she was about to apply nail varnish. It didn't even look like the moles you see on the chart. But better safe than sorry. The nail was removed, the offending clump of melanocytes excised and tested.

The test results were not good.

Acral lentiginous melanoma. Not benign. Malignant. Dangerous. Potentially lethal, that tiny little blot. It's not related to sun exposure, so there was no blame on her (or us). Still, tests showed that it had spread to a lymph node on the foot. A sentinel node, that's what they call them. Watching out for trouble. If that's infected, then the next stage is worse. Stage III, they call it, like some tricky examination. Maths, Further Maths, Much Further Maths. Catherine had her entire lymph node basin removed from her foot and ankle. Basin – it's a good description for what is an entire river system, carrying white blood cells to where they are needed, and taking toxins away. But hiding away amongst the toxins are cancerous cells, still alive. She was 38, and she was very brave about it. When under local anaesthetic she watched them peel back her creamy skin, remove the nodes, then stitch it almost invisibly back. The next nodes, the next basin, seemed to be uninfected. It was then a question of waiting. Cancer's Russian roulette. That was when the question of having a child became more urgent. As she always said to me: 'That's what I was made for. To bring a new life into the world.'

And to protect it, Catherine. Against all the badness this world can throw at you. That's why you survived cancer, Catherine. You have a job to do. I can't help you now. No one can help you. It's your task alone. I know the date and the time, and the place. But I can't come back and warn you. God, how I wish that I could.

Tuesday. Almost eight in the morning, and she has to leave for work in half an hour. I've just finished getting Ethan up. Catherine is doing pilates, lying in the centre of the lounge listening to the CD, whose soft rainforest music is full of bird calls and pattering raindrops. Because of the time, she hasn't bothered to put her leggings and leotard on. She's just wearing shorts and an old T-shirt with a faint orange stain on one side that, I am now experienced enough to be sure, is baby vomit. The voice on the CD, all mid-Atlantic vowels and breathy enthusiasm, is enjoining her to be aware of her own body, its balance and alignment. 'Make sure you are square-aware, and *breathe, breathe* in until you have expanded your ribcage to its maximum. Now hold it gently, and make a few slow pelvic tilts.'

Mindfulness seems out of reach though. She eyes me staring at her, and starts giggling. 'Don't. You know I can't concentrate if you watch.' More giggling. But I stay leaning in the doorway, my arms folded, a slight grin on my face as I listen to Ethan's happy burbling from the bedroom. Her hips tilt, her tummy flattens, the puke patch creases. I see the tell-tale vibration in her diaphragm. Silent laughter.

'Right, that's it!' She jumps up and chases me around the lounge. I let her catch me by the kitchen door, and she tickles me quite hard in the ribs. As I mock up a wounded expression, she stands on tiptoes to give me a slow languorous kiss. 'Tonight. I promise. He'll sleep better, even if I have to have a G&T before I feed him,' she whispers.

'You are going to drug our precious child?' I say in faux horror.

She smiles and licks my neck. It's a delicious feeling. 'Maybe.'

I did get that promised act of lovemaking on Tuesday night.

It was wonderful.

It was my last.

Chapter Two

Wednesday. There are poignant moments from the start of that terrible day. It's 8.30. I've just come down from the bathroom, and I see there has been something of a breakfast incident. Catherine is in the kitchen holding the remains of a pot of yoghurt. She's bending over, sweetly dishevelled, and looking meaningfully at Ethan in his high chair. There is yoghurt all around Ethan's mouth, on the plastic tray, and speckled on the floor. Catherine puts her little finger in a yoghurt smear on his tray, and paints the goop around her own mouth. Ethan explodes in chuckles, and repeatedly bangs his plastic teaspoon on the tray in appreciation of this mimicry.

'Messy Mummy,' Catherine says, before putting the finger in her mouth. 'Mmm. Fairtrade sugar-free tropical fruit flavour, all the milk from certified happy cows. Do you want some, Ethan?'

Ethan bangs his spoon again, spattering yoghurt liberally. He loses his grip on the upstroke. The spoon sails over his shoulder, and a vanilla blob lands in Catherine's hair. We all laugh. I wish I'd had a camera. But never mind. I'll remember it for ever. Good memories are an insulation. They help cushion the blows of life.

Even of death.

Later on Wednesday but still in Manchester. Same city, different world. Maybe two miles from where we live, a young man stirs to a not-very-new day in a basement flat that reeks of socks, booze, fags and weed. It's eleven o'clock. He's wreathed in grey sheets that haven't been washed since God knows when. His shaven head is half under a pillow, a twisted mouth snoring. More visible is a protruding shoulder, a muscled hillock of indigo and viridian, entwined foliage around a dagger, blade upwards and the initials tattooed beneath in gothic script, MSM on his pale, freckled skin. The floor is strewn with clothes. There are cans too: Carling, Red Bull, Bulmer's, Coke. He's not fussy, so long as it supplies the effect he's looking for. Look around and you see crisp packets, biscuit wrappers, a half-eaten pizza slice, a KFC box. In a heap by a huge TV, boxes for video games: *Carmageddon*, *Dark Souls III*, *Dead Rising*.

Don't get me wrong. This is not a drug den. There isn't a single crystal of crack cocaine in the place, nor a syringe. Liam generally gets his buzz and his stupefaction, his energy intake and his entertainment, from familiar sources. In that respect he's like the rest of us, only more so. I'd slid back a few days to take a closer look at him, and how he lived, given how we were going to get to know him, Catherine, Ethan and I. The animal purity and immediacy of his impulses are almost beautiful.

He's a single-minded jaguar for the urban jungle. Thirsty, get a can. Hungry, go to KFC or Mickey D's. Tired, get a Red Bull. Bored, slay some zombies. Angry. Yeah, every day there was anger. Well, the outlets for that were legion. Usually indulged fraternally, with the rest of the nocturnal tribe.

Liam Fretwell is a gang criminal of course, and the flat belongs to the gang. For a supposedly successful con, there's only one thing missing, and that's money. He has just 15 quid in his jeans pocket, a few coins on the floor. He's on the run from prison, but that doesn't worry him. What does bother him is that he's skint, and he hates being skint. It's a personal affront to his standing, his status and prestige. He knows who to blame. Sparko Sinclair. Today's the day when that score gets settled.

His eyes are opening. They are a startling icy blue, set in a skin almost as pale as Catherine's. He has a malevolent pucker between his dark eyebrows, and a short but deep scar along the side of his nose from a Stanley knife wound. That was from his first landing altercation at HMP Wakefield, seven years ago, when he was 19. It looks nasty, but as he would always say, you should have seen the other guy.

I want to understand Liam Fretwell.

He was a one-year-old once, probably a yoghurt thrower, I don't know. Probably chucked stones too, a little later. I can't go back that far, or get that level of detail. But I know this. Something clicked early in that cascading interconnection of genetics and environment that turned him into a monster. Yet he wasn't one of those offspring who would be easy to predict on that trajectory. He had parents, two of 'em, both present for his childhood. No abuse on the record. No domestic violence. An older brother, Steven, who became a joiner, and now makes posh kitchens for big houses in Wilmslow. His own business, doing well.

But not Liam. Something there inside him, something wrong, something twisted and nasty. A kind of carcinogenic mole of the soul. Neither sought out nor excised. A lump of resentment gone bad. What was initially an indifference to the pain and suffering of others became by late teenage years a little kick of pleasure, a pulse of power. The first flexings of intimidation helped that nodule of badness crystallise into evil.

Back to us. On that damp Wednesday in April. The puddles from the last shower are drying on the tarmac. (I will get to see a close-up of that tarmac, believe me.) Reliving it, I'm now getting tetchy about not being able to warn her. I mean, there was really no reason why it had to be that day that we drove to Manchester Royal Infirmary, on her monthly appointment to see the Mole People, as she called them. And those dermatologists do indeed reside underground, in an absurdly overheated linoleum-lined basement that smells of hot dust and disinfectant. If we'd known about the dangers of today, we could have asked for a new appointment. There are always cancellations. The good old NHS will always cheerily put you back in the queue. It's what they do. It's no good me thinking about that now. It happened. The day was set. That Wednesday made sense for Catherine because the computer system at her work was being upgraded. 'It's always useless for half a day afterwards, and I can't bear to hear Helen whinging about her emails for the rest of the day.' She laughed, that lovely infectious chuckle. 'I'd just rather be somewhere else. Anywhere else.'

Yes, she certainly ended up somewhere else. And so did I.

Life-changing days hide in with the others, like jokers in a pack of cards. Imposters in the weekly roll-call of trivia and tedium. We were preparing for the hated Asda run to Hulme, a necessary chore on the way back from the Mole People. I'd just paid the council tax, Catherine had rung her mother. The babysitter had let us down, so Ethan had to come with us. Then there were Bags for Life, batteries to recycle, a long once-a-month list of the stuff you can't get at Aldi. I mean we're only talking tinned prunes and coconut milk, bales of cheap toilet roll, that kind of thing. But there was the Moss Side deli to visit too. Well, that was what we called it. It had some Asian name with initials. KG Stores, I think, on Claremont Road. It was the highlight of any food shopping trip for me, not that there was much competition. But the Moss Side deli supplies wonders that we can't get anywhere else locally. Ready-made dolmades with vine leaves. Fresh okra for ladyfinger curry or for Cajun cuisine. Sweet potato, fresh curry leaves, soft Kurdish cheese in huge tins. That is all my department. I'm the house husband. Travel the world in 80 tastes. I love to cook for her. Well, I did. Can't any more of course.

But that's why we are where we are. Parked on Walton Road, just round the corner from KG Stores, in the middle of Moss Side, at 4.03 p.m. on Wednesday 12 April. Caught up in the biggest spree killing in Manchester's history.

I am in the shop, you see, when it happens. Immersed in the smell of spices: the heady garam masala, the sweet cakey dust of cinnamon, the tang of cumin. A little bit of the exotic East. So I don't see what happens outside at the time. I know *now* of course. I know everything now. That comes of being where I am now. That knowledge is a kind of privilege, but it's frustrating too. To be able to watch over her, but not to hold her hand, not to kiss her. To know what she's thinking, but not to be able to let her know what I'm thinking. Not to be able to tell her that I love her. Not to be able to comfort. That hurts, honestly it does. Because there is so much to tell her, now I know it all.

The first I know is the sound of a car revving. I glance up, and out into the street. The beige Nissan, our little Nissan with the missing front left hubcap. On the far side a bulky man-shape that I would later know to be Liam Fretwell is in the driving seat. My seat! And a tall, skinny Afro-Caribbean man has the front passenger door open, a blink of an eye, and he's in. Our car. My little boy, one year old in a week's time, would be in his little car seat. And where is Catherine? All this I take in instantly.

I drop everything and just sprint. I have a clear run through the shop doorway. I'm bellowing Catherine's name, and everyone just shrinks back to let me pass. I'm not beefy, I'm not threatening, but I am tall. Six-four. Anger looks odd on me. Like a furious giraffe. The Nissan is pulling a U-turn, tyres screeching, which gives me two seconds to decide what to do before it passes back in front of me towards Princess Road.

I can make Catherine out. I can see she is in the back by the corona of golden sunlight around her hair, and I can see

11

her protective arm around the child seat. Her stance instantly telegraphs that Ethan is in it, even though he's too low for me to see. The front passenger has turned round towards her, an arm outstretched, rigid. And I can see the driver, now on my side, his merciless taut face and his thick, tattooed arms. He stares at me, and seems to know what I am already committed to doing. The only meaningful option.

I sprint out into the road, heedless of the traffic, and throw myself headlong onto the bonnet of our car. The bang as I hit the windscreen puts me face to face with them both for the first time.

Fretwell and Cousins.

On the day in question, Liam Fretwell, 26, an enforcer for the Moss Side Mafia, is busy. He's being sought by the police and on the run from prison, but has already found time for two murders. The first was planned. Frankie 'Sparko' Sinclair. Sparko is, no let me correct myself, *was* a sad case: a disabled alcoholic and small-time crook who had been Fretwell's former neighbour and drinking partner. To be an associate of Fretwell's was Sparko's last, deadly descent on a slow slide of bad luck. A former Royal Signals corporal, he had served in Iraq, but after discharge couldn't cope. Violent outbursts, a conviction for domestic abuse, a broken marriage, periods of drug dependency, alcoholism, some jail time and occasional homelessness.

Several years earlier, in a different life, I had actually been Sinclair's probation officer. Considering he only had one leg and was confined to a wheelchair, he led me a merry dance. But for all that I don't think he deserved what Fretwell did to him.

Nobody deserves that.

The biggest surprise about Sparko, I suppose, is that such a fourth-division low life got himself into such premier league trouble. Everyone in my district knew about Fretwell. He already had a reputation, even at 17, when I was still in the probation service and overheard the conversations. A man to make anyone quiver. Two years later he was sentenced to life, with a tariff of 14 years, for the torture and killing of two members of a rival drug gang, and the theft of their loot. It was a significant sum, more than 2 million in various currencies which the RHC22 gang had snatched from a hold-up at a bureau de change in the Arndale Shopping Centre, and a hoard of amphetamines. None of it was ever recovered. Fretwell was a classic category 'A' prisoner: violent, disruptive and incapable of good behaviour. The word recidivism might have been invented for him. There was no way that he was going to be allowed the kind of early release that is available to those prisoners who show signs of remorse and rehabilitation. Fretwell had been determined to escape, but HMP Wakefield is not the easiest of jails to get out of. Only one person has done so in its entire history, and that was in 1959.

Still, there are ways. Fretwell collapsed in his cell at two a.m. on Sunday morning, screaming for help. He complained of unbearable pains in his abdomen. The prison's duty medic was called and, after examining him and given the location of the pain, feared that Fretwell had peritonitis. He signed off for him to be taken to the nearest Accident and Emergency department, at Pinderfields Hospital, just a couple of miles away. Prison Service regulations stipulate that any category 'A' prisoner should be accompanied by at least four prison officers outside the grounds. Given the prison service recruitment crisis, the regulations are of course a complete fantasy. That was as many officers as the entire prison had for a weekend night shift. So Fretwell was accompanied in the ambulance by just two officers and, despite the protestations of the two paramedics, was handcuffed to the gurney on which he lay, writhing in apparent agony.

The main entrance to HMP Wakefield is in the city centre, on the inappropriately named Love Lane, an area of old warehouses and industrial estate adjoining the main railway line. At precisely 2.52 a.m., after picking up Fretwell but before the ambulance had even crossed back into Parliament Street, it was rammed by a stolen car, and brought to a halt. As the paramedics emerged to check if the driver was injured two masked men from a third vehicle held them up at gunpoint. One of the assailants tied up the paramedics and put them in the stolen car, the other opened the back of the ambulance. The prison officers were forced to release Fretwell, and then tied up too. The prisoner, pausing only to repeatedly stamp on the head of one officer he particularly disliked, was whisked away by his fellow gang members. Fretwell was back in hiding in Manchester in two hours.

It was without doubt the most precisely organised event that Fretwell had ever been involved in, though the credit, if that is the right word, should go not to him but to the brains at the top of the Moss Side Mafia. Fretwell reckoned Sparko owed him money. A lot of money, and presumably the gang was in for a cut if they helped spring him from jail.

Fretwell was at Sparko's address on Walton Road, Moss Side, by two o'clock on Monday. He knew it well. He used to live on the first floor until his jailing seven years ago. Sparko had lived below, in the wheelchair accessible ground-floor flat. There was nothing remarkable about it. It was part of a 1960s purpose-built block, six flats, two on each floor. It was originally council owned, then sold off to a housing association which struggled to keep on top of the maintenance. It fitted right in with the depressed urban milieu of Moss Side: the satellite dishes, the abandoned settee in the front yard of an adjacent house, the scattered wheelie bins, the litter, the row of nearby shops with graffitied roller shutters.

Fretwell turned the place over, smashed it up good and proper, but there was no sign of Sparko or the money.

Now, about Sparko Sinclair. Put yourself in his position. Fretwell was not a man you would double cross, even when he was inside, given his gangland connections. But if you heard he was out and gunning for you, then it really would be time to hide. Sparko must have been psychic. He must have heard within the day of Fretwell's escape. Maybe it was someone on the inside at Wakefield, tipping him the knowledge. Whatever it was, Sparko vanished. Quite an impressive feat for a one-legged man confined to a wheelchair.

Fretwell spent the next 24 hours chucking Sparko's name around the streets, bouncing it around the mates, the bruvs and the boys, hoping for a useful echo. Then he got lucky. Janile Cousins, another of the Moss Side crew, supplied the occasional bag of cannabis to the single mum who now occupied Fretwell's old flat. Lorraine Caldwell told Janile that Sparko had left in a hurry by taxi on Monday evening. She was glad about it because, as she put it: 'He was a minging pisshead.' But she had no idea where he'd gone.

All this was just round the corner, three doors down from KG Stores where next day I would be picking through the Kurdish delicacies for my beloved Catherine. Those delicacies which would end up in the bin; uncooked, unprepared, forgotten. Three doors and 20 yards separated two worlds: one of delicious, exotic food, the other which would on that fateful Wednesday turn out to be the site of an unprovoked murder by Fretwell and Cousins, their second killing of that day and by no means the last.

A busy day for death.

Janile Cousins, now there's a story. A Jamaican mother, no known father, and a life lived mostly in the urine-stained stairwell of Block B, Palmerston Fields. The one tower where the lights were always broken between floors 10 and 14, and where the lift had never worked for more than a day at a time. A small but significant no-go area on which the council had given up. Janile, known as Jazzer, had two older sisters. Letitia, the first, went to college. Left Moss Side and never came back. She was the success, the one social workers smiled about. Eleesha was younger, and went off the rails pretty quickly.

Staying out all night. Drugs, bad boys. And it was one of those boys who drew Janile into the world of gangs. His first job was as a runner: delivering, receiving. Then he was to hold a shooter which he kept at the bottom of a box of dirty mags under his bed, ready for the call on the burner phone they had given him. But Jazzer Cousins had a weakness for girls. He ended up running the pass-arounds for the Moss Side Mafia. The drug-addicted teenagers who were kept available for gang leaders, and the best-looking of whom were offered as tribute when meeting the Albanians, the suppliers of choice.

Now, back to the main event.

It took until the afternoon of the next day, Wednesday, for Fretwell and Cousins to find out where Sparko had moved to. It was just a few miles away. Probably another tip-off on the gangland grapevine, or maybe they tracked down the taxi driver. We'll probably never know. Fretwell did the damage to Sparko that he planned, and quickly, because he knew he had to be. But five minutes of torture is still a long time, I think you'd agree. Lit cigarettes, eyelids, testicles. You see what I'm saying. Sparko must have told them what they wanted to hear, because they were back at Walton Road in a few minutes. There, they smashed in the skull of Lorraine Caldwell, their informant, in front of her two-year-old daughter and left her body on the stairs. That's what they thought of motherhood. But then they were hot on the trail of Fretwell's missing money. It was a gory trail, too.

By 3.40 p.m., Sparko was dead.

By 3.50 p.m., Lorraine Caldwell was dead.

Twenty minutes later I'd be joining them.

So how did I get to be there, at that moment? It was all decided years earlier. You could say that Catherine had hunted me down. She wrote the spec, she researched the means, scanned the possibilities, checked every detail, locked on, and closed in for the kill. I was a project. She told me all about it, though not for years afterwards. The Husband Project. Planned and executed. Perhaps not on time, but certainly within budget.

Catherine hadn't had a lot of luck with men. There had been boyfriends of course. Her figure guaranteed an interest, especially from a distance. Catherine was busty, something I liked from the start, but she hated. 'For my whole adult life I've been forced to carry around a billboard which always attracts one kind of man, the last type I'm actually looking for,' she once said. That was why she practised what she called defensive dressing: trousers rather than skirts, lowish heels, but crucially two or more colourful ethnic scarves looped loosely over whatever blouse or top she was wearing. Urban camouflage. By the time she met me she'd been dressing defensively for years, and her conclusion was that it led men's eyes back up to her face. As a result she was listened to, her opinions were more valued, and she was respected. That's not very scientific of course. I didn't tell her that, because I learned early on never to challenge her most strongly held views. But my own feeling was that self-worth came as much from the inside as the outside. The process of building self-respect and identity. She was constructing the Catherine that she wanted to be. Growing up, you could say. But a lifetime isn't long enough to grow up completely. It's certainly not long enough to be ready for the worst that can happen. Nothing can prepare you for that. Because these things are not meant to be part of your life. Born, childhood, school, college, job, marriage, kids, and retirement. Where does violent abduction fit in that list? It doesn't. It belongs to someone else's life. Someone like Fretwell's.

Only there's a snag.

Fretwell's life has collided with ours. Mayhem has smashed into order. And there are casualties.

It's ten to four and I'm still in the deli. Catherine is kneeling on the back seat of the Nissan, one foot sticking out of the open door, as she reaches down into the footwell below Ethan. The boy has dropped Lugs again and is working up for a squall, his tiny ash-blond eyebrows knitted in frustration. 'Oh Ethan, be nice to Lugs. He doesn't like to be dropped on his head,' Catherine says. She grasps the saliva-soggy rabbit when she hears shouting outside. She turns to see two men, one black, one white, both oozing menace. They are circling round a battered blue Vauxhall parked a few spaces back. Violent recriminations are hurled between them about the keys that each claims the other possesses.

Catherine hears it, but what she doesn't know is that they've just committed a murder, their second of the day, and they need to get out of there, fast. But without keys, they can't.

'That's a lot of Fs and Cs, isn't it Ethan?' she whispers as she rests her face against the child and presses the now retrieved Lugs into the boy's tiny fingers. Suddenly frightened, she turns and pulls the rear door closed behind her. It gives a satisfying clunk. Come on Geoff, she thinks. Hurry up. I need you here. She wonders about the car keys dangling vulnerably in the Nissan's steering column, a long reach away. The central locking button is closer, but would it work without the ignition on?

There is a brief silence, the sound of running, two impacts and suddenly there are two men in the front seats of her car. 'Hey, what do you think you're...' she begins.

The engine roars into life. The passenger, the black guy, turns dead eyes to her and pulls a gun from the inside of his puffa jacket. He points it right at her. 'Shut it, sister,' he says.

The car sets off like a racer, and they are immediately screeching a U-turn in the side road beyond the deli. I am sprinting out of the shop towards her side of the vehicle, screaming at them to stop. Mesmerised, Catherine watches as I launch myself at the vehicle. She hears the impact, and sees me splayed horizontally across the windscreen, hanging on to the wipers. I hear her screaming at them. 'Stop, stop, stop,' she yells, over the ululation of distress coming from Ethan. She knows, for sure, what is going to happen to me. She has seen the gun in Cousins' hand, though I have not. But then neither of us knew about the other weapon, the cruder, crueller but equally deadly tool that is Fretwell's speciality.

He had a name for what he does with it.

Wetwork.

Chapter Three

The night before, Catherine had been lying awake. I sensed the shallowness of her breath, the sighing and the turning, which drew me out of a deeper sleep. I slid my arm around her, nestled into the warm curve of her and whispered: 'What are you thinking about, love?' She told me that she was wondering about where the spare office security key had gone. She'd been fretting about it since the weekend. Kelly Harris, her boss, had let her have it so she could come in on Sunday to finish up some online training. She had returned it to the key cupboard on Monday, but now it was missing. Kelly was blaming her. A lost key meant a £250 deposit forfeited to the property company.

I knew the key wasn't really the issue. It was much bigger than that. She'd been on edge about her job for months. Another round of restructuring was in train, initiated by a cut in funding by the local authority. Four years earlier, she'd already endured the ignominy of having to reapply for her own job. Actually, not her own job, but what turned out to be a worse position with even less money. It just happened to include all her old responsibilities plus some new ones. No car allowance anymore. The separate training allowance and the five days a year she used to get to take extra training, that went too. She is still required to get the training ('mandated' is the word they used – it's *mandatory*). But she is now expected to do this in her own time.

Catherine used to be a Senior Education and Skills Project Officer. Now she's no longer 'senior' even though the policy chief above her has been made redundant, and his supposedly senior work has cascaded down to her. Still, at least she has a job. She was successful in her reapplication. Hoo-bleeding-ray. Amy, the other SESPO, wasn't. Catherine joked that as the only one, she was now the 'it' in SESPIT. Two out of the seven in the rank below her in her department didn't survive the cull either. But naturally there was still the same amount of work as before. It was just spread over fewer staff.

If I could have earned more money, then perhaps she wouldn't have been quite so anxious. But then I was trying to combine my freelance website design role with being a 'home dad'. I suggest you try it, if you think it's easy. It was hard to take client calls when Ethan was crying. And wouldn't you guess it, the one sound that always set him off was the telephone. So to keep my clients, I made sure I was cheap. And actually, to be fair, being cheap was right, because I was not that good. I overlooked things. I was tired a lot. I was crabby and impatient. Clients didn't like it. But so long as I was cheap, I kept most of them. And there was never so much work that I had to register for VAT, so I could always compete with the big boys on price.

These are the daily battles we all have, right? Legitimate worries, fair enough. Quite enough to keep you awake at night, if you don't have anything bigger to worry about. I feel guilty as hell about all of it, the stuff I could have done, how I could have helped. If I had worked harder, if she hadn't had to balance so many demands on her time. If that Wednesday hadn't been the only convenient day to get the hospital appointment. If something tiny could have been different, then everything would have been different. Catherine and Ethan wouldn't have had to go through what they went through.

And I wouldn't be dead.

Fretwell accelerates hard, with me still stuck on the windscreen like a giant bug. What he can see of the road above my sliding legs I have no idea. I'm hanging on to those good solid Nissan wipers. He screeches round a corner, and my legs flip round until my feet are over the radiator, but still I hang on. Then he turns sharply and stamps on the brakes, and we slide sideways to a halt by a zebra crossing. It's at that point that I spin off on the driver's side, one wiper blade coming off in my hand. I glimpse a Belisha beacon, its faint orange flash a warning, as I scramble dizzily to my feet. I detect Ethan's wailing from inside the car, then proclaimed in full volume as Fretwell throws opens the driver's side door. I hear Catherine's ragged voice calling my name.

He's got a knife in his hand: narrow, pointed and – though I don't see this at the time – it's already smeared with dried blood from Sparko Sinclair. Fretwell is swearing and shouting at me, and he's very, very fast. I'm on my feet, just, but I don't have a second to get away. Just time to bring my arms up between us. Pure instinct. I've not had to defend myself since school, and never against a knife. But for Fretwell, it's just another bit of wetwork. He's past my defences in the blink of an eye, and again I hear Catherine: 'No, leave him alone, oh God, NO, NO, NO.' Then her scream.

Let me tell you what it's like being stabbed.

It begins with an embrace, a stranger's left arm around your shoulder, holding you close even as you try to block the blow. Then the terrible, penetrating intimacy of that low, pistoning right arm. Seven, eight, nine quick abdominal thrusts. Burning hot and cold, sutures of death stitch into your gut. Then the splitting and the spilling and the sudden flash flood of blood. As he releases me, I search my fogging vision for my wife and my son through that windscreen. I can hear their screams. All I want is a last look. But all I can make out in the hard bright sunlight is my own gore-spattered reflection. I open my mouth to call my undying love to Catherine, and with my last breath on this earth spray my life out on the bonnet of our car, like scattering rose petals at a wedding.

The next moment I'm ejected from my own body, soaring above myself, hundreds of feet in the cool, damp air. A posthumous Google Earth. Toybox Manchester spills below me, a tantrum of russet and grey Lego bricks spread from horizon to horizon. This living, pulsing city, threaded with busy roads, the Old Trafford Stadium to the north-west, the ship canal way out west, and the city centre with its high rises. Two and a half million people, alive, riding their ordinary days while I traverse the first few seconds of the hereafter. I've done this in dreams, many times. Felt the vertigo even in sleep, the blissful freedom and the power to control my disembodied self.

But this isn't joy, it's death. And let me tell you, there is no majestic celestial escalator to a light above. I'm not ready for this, there is work to do below. There's my family to save. I cannot bear to be separated from Catherine and Ethan. I dive back down again, towards our blood-sheened vehicle. Fretwell is kicking my lanky, limp body over on the asphalt, clear of the wheels. Then he stamps on my head for good measure. There's a ring of bystanders, some from shops, some from other vehicles, some waiting to cross the road, all just standing and staring in horror. After what they've seen, they're all too frightened even to be seen bringing out a phone for a pic. Fretwell is back in the car now, and they're off, shooting down Westbridge Road, twice the speed of anything else. It seems not to be of my own volition, but I swoop and accelerate, then 'pop'– I'm in the car with Catherine and Ethan. She's as white as bone, trembling, her mouth open. Cousins has the gun trained on her and says:

'Don't you ever scream again, okay?' he turns to his mate. 'What are we going to do with 'em, Fretty?'

'Fucking kill 'em. But not here. Chuck 'em out somewhere quiet, before we get the next set of wheels. Can't see a fucking thing through this.' He indicates the speckled screen, where a coin-sized dollop of my blood, edges scalloped like a bottle cap, squats reproachfully in the centre of his vision. The Nissan is spattered with me: bonnet, radiator, and most inconveniently, windscreen. Fretwell is cursing because in one of my final and perhaps under-appreciated achievements, I had broken off the driver's side wiper blade and bent the other. My epitaph – *Geoffrey Blake: Loving husband and father, not so easily eradicated from this earth.*

Unsighted or not, Fretwell accelerates past a Royal Mail van, passing on the wrong side of a pedestrian refuge. An elderly man waiting to cross stares in amazement. Catherine is embracing our crying child, stroking Ethan's soft, downy hair. His breath is coming in great shudders. He's distressed and confused and probably a little car-sick. Catherine shushes and hugs, and with her spare hand is nervously trying to tighten his straps, though she herself has no seatbelt on. But her survival brain, operating beyond grief and terror, wonders if she could reach her phone, which is in a bag by her feet. It was switched off at the hospital, because she's good like that. She respects rules, because there do have to be rules. She didn't remember putting it back on. If the phone is off it would be good, because if it rings they might just kill her there and then without a second thought.

Ethan looks up at her, with Lugs in his tiny fist, and asks: 'Dadda?'

Where is Daddy?

It is at that moment that the fear-cinched binding that has held in all her emotions finally gives way. Tears slide down her face, and she jams a fist into her mouth, pressing her teeth into her knuckles to prevent the wail of abject loss that is building inside her.

She looks up and sees Fretwell's knotted ugly face in the mirror. 'Don't you start, right? I don't want to hear a fucking word out of you.'

She wants to say: 'You've killed him. It took all my life to find him, and you've taken him away from me.' But she says nothing.

Good girl.

School hadn't been great for Catherine. She wasn't a good girl then, not particularly. Grew up in Leeds, went to the local comprehensive. Middling academic achievement, a bent towards sciences and maths. Not pretty in those years, not sporty, bigger built than most, but not by much. Labelled 'carrot-top', 'milk bottle' or 'Titselina' by her classmates. She had enough street wisdom not to make herself stand out in any other way. Mucking about in class to fit in. She confessed to a little bit of verbal bullying of those even less popular than she was. Still, she always felt on the outside. Two good friends saved her. A clever and spunky Asian girl called Sabina, who eventually went to the London School of Economics and became a City economist, and Megan, a shrewd and intelligent girl who cloaked her own teenage vulnerability in an acidic cynicism. Megan married early, had three quick kids, and remains a mum in Leeds. She is still Catherine's best friend, and has been invaluable during her long struggle to bring a child into the world.

Catherine didn't expect to go to university, but by the time she was in the sixth form her self-confidence and exam results had improved. She got a place on a management studies course at

Keele. She was much happier there than at school, and the fact that the course was dull didn't matter. She suddenly discovered a talent: organising others, with tact, diplomacy and humour. That is how she ended up in the management of education and skills. This culminated in FuturePerfectSkills, one of those precarious half-in half-out public–private organisations, or stakeholder partnerships, as its directors prefer to call it. FPS relies on government money, and is embedded within a local authority structure, but often has to find a lot of its own cash for important projects. FPS is jam-packed with bright, well-meaning, liberal individuals, immersed in issues like race, gender and diversity. A very political workplace. Especially since the cutbacks.

She is very good at navigating that minefield. Emotional intelligence, maturity, unflappability. I could recognise a lot of qualities she had that I did not. She spends a lot of time defusing issues, brokering compromise, incentivising and above all communicating. It helps that she is dealing with rational, intelligent, if overly principled, individuals. You can appeal to a common conception of progress, however differently interpreted.

But what about those skills in different circumstances? When no world view is shared, when a plan is what happens in the next half minute, when an incentive is communicated through the barrel of a gun, pressed to your head. When it's life and death. What then?

You listen. You think fast. And you say nothing.

She learns that very quickly. But then she is a very smart woman.

Chapter Four

Catherine had never seen a real gun. And now she is staring down the barrel of one. Black, slick with sweat and oil, scratched, and rather bigger than she'd expected. It's two feet away, held low between the seats so those in other vehicles cannot see it. The hand that holds it, a left hand, has long caramel-coloured fingers, chocolate-dark creases at the knuckle, each digit ending in a fat, curved and unbitten nail. They are never still, quite, even the tightly curved one in the trigger. Each wriggle, each flexing, could be the one that discharges the weapon. Each twitch of the speeding car, each turn, makes the barrel wave, pointing either at her or at Ethan. She realises how much more she trembles when it is at Ethan. If it comes to it, make it me, not him, she thinks. Please, just make it me. That is what my wife is thinking.

The face above the weapon is devoid of recognition, of warmth, of empathy. The man whose name she does not yet know is twisted round in the passenger seat to keep an eye on her. He has a medusa-like hairstyle, which waves with the movement of the car. It's a cap of short dreadlocks on top, razor-cut round the sides and back, and a sparse ill-kempt beard. The pale brown eyes are bloodshot, the whites slightly yellowish. His breath is sour and unpleasant. She wonders if he is on drugs, and concludes that the answer is probably yes.

She concentrates on softening the muscles in her face, trying to free her clenched jaw. Relax the TMJ – it was something in her pilates CD. She didn't know what TMJ stood for. But she needs to do it. Ease down the tension all round. She rehearses a slight smile, a hesitant stretching of her mouth, showing her even white teeth, an attempt to make eye contact. He looks right through her.

Her opening gambit is one that would work on any normal human, anyone who has even a scintilla of empathy.

'This is Ethan,' she says softly, gesturing at her son.

Cousins ignores her.

Ethan, hearing his own name, turns to look at his mother. His eyes are wide open, so blue, so radiantly, heartbreakingly, innocent. He searches her face, looking for the anguish which she was so recently forced to extinguish. What made Mummy shout and cry? She smiles wanly at him, and strokes his soft, downy hair and absorbs the warm biscuity smell of him. Reassured, Ethan now turns to look at Janile Cousins, stretches his tiny arm and offers him Lugs. The child makes a sound which could be 'ugs' or 'hugs' but is probably meant to be Lugs, and is accompanied by a thread of drool that spills down the front of his bib. The furry rabbit, held out towards the enemy, stares down the barrel of the gun.

Catherine watches intently for signs that this gesture has been noticed.

Janile Cousins eyes flick to the child, only for a second, and he repositions the weapon a little further away. It no longer points directly at either Catherine or Ethan. More like between them.

It's a microscopic change.

But it feels like a victory.

I first saw Catherine on a dating website on 15 September 2012. They weren't then quite as sophisticated as they are now. I was 37, recently divorced, and a bit lonely. I'd been a probation officer, but after a dozen years of increasing frustration had given it up to become a freelance website designer. I don't know why I had ever thought this would bring in enough money, but believe me, if you've worked for the Ministry of Justice for a few years, you'd gladly take any job that offers a bit of freedom. Working from home was great, at first, but after my first wife Laura and I broke up, it wasn't so great. I had started drinking, for all the wrong reasons. So that's why I was on a dating website in 2012.

I liked Catherine's profile from the start. I loved the big hair, the broad smile. The photograph showed her in an outdoor setting, crossing a stile in frosty woodland, hills in the background. Big jacket and scarf, of course. Outdoors, that was a big plus. She mentioned hill walking, so we had one activity in common, anyway. There was no mention of mountain biking, or fell-running, where I had begun to sublimate my own frustration and loneliness in the last couple of years. Still, can't expect miracles. The blurb on her profile didn't give too much away. Career girl, got the house, the car and a great circle of friends. Just needs the right man. That sort of thing. Fairly standard, right?

I sent her a message, and quickly got a brief but chatty reply. I sent her another message and then waited a week for an answer. What I eventually found out was that she was crunching through an awful lot of other candidates. Internet dating: it's a numbers game in the end, so the initial pool she set herself was broad. A hundred non-smoking degree-level guys, ideally neither pierced nor tattooed, in the 30 to 45 age range, based anywhere within reasonable driving distance from her home in Wythenshawe. That range encompassed most of Greater Manchester, and parts of Cheshire. Once tagged, she would then message them through the website, rather than wait to hear, as many women do. Those early messages were initially chatty, but carried a standard text towards the end. She wanted to know what was really important to them in another person. She was hoping to read some key words: loyalty, reliability, supportiveness, listening. Often what she got back was a lot of specifics: must be up for Saturday nights out, must support Man U (or some other club), must enjoy curry. There was a lot of barely concealed macho, a lot of self-aggrandisement. She showed me some of the responses. A lot of fragile egos. It's amazing how easily you can spot them.

That still left a lot of men who were giving out the right signals. The next essential test in Project Husband was the phone call. She was surprised how many men weren't comfortable with a long phone conversation. From a message or two on the site, they wanted to text, or email, or move straight on to a date. For her it was vital to hear them in real time: the breath, the laughter, the verbal cadences, timbre and accent, all so freighted with the human soul.

Her call to me was on 24 September. A Sunday. I knew it was her, even before I picked up the phone. 'Is that Geoff?' Her voice was breathy, hesitant. It seemed small and faraway.

'Yes,' I said. 'That's Catherine, isn't it?' I wasn't taking any chances here. I was a newbie.

I'd only shared my number with one other woman from the site, Wendy, and I certainly wasn't expecting a call from her.

There was a lot of nervous laughter from both of us as Catherine wondered whether I would be in, or out on my mountain bike in the drizzle. I told her I wasn't that rufty-tufty. 'I really don't like the rain on my glasses,' I said. 'It's really annoying.'

She then explained how she had contact lenses, and we passed a very easy ten minutes on the tribulation of lenses versus glasses, not exchanging any significant information, but merely meshing ourselves into a comfortable conversation. Two cogs where the teeth didn't clash, but fitted snugly, oiled by humour: speak, listen, laugh, speak, listen, laugh and so on. A precursor to more testing topics.

I then wheeled out one of only three rehearsed conversational gambits I had prepared. It was a longish and richly illustrated tale from when I was a child of ten. I had been staying at an aunt's farm and had gone off cycling in the country and got a puncture, and pushed the bike back in the rain for four miles in what turned out to be the wrong direction, before a kindly lady I met rang the farm and I was given a lift. I wanted her to imagine the appealing little boy. It's a harmless story I had enjoyed success with before, with Laura, my ex, amongst others. It had all the right ingredients: a little self-deprecation and a little self-knowledge. Find the child still in the man. It seemed to work with Catherine too.

The dynamics of a conversation can be planned, up to a point, whether it's a date, a job interview, a staff review, or even a dispute. Where do you start? Common ground, of course. That's why we Brits usually begin with the weather, something we all have to endure. Common ground and empathy; uncontroversial. Catherine was very good at it. She'd learned and she had a good instinct.

Now, in this speeding car, she was trying to begin the hardest conversation of her life. With one of the men who had just five minutes ago killed her husband. There was no common ground there. Killing me had been a casual necessity for them, a grievous loss for her. Some deep survival part of her recognised that now was not the time to reflect on what she had just lost, enormous though it was. Now was a time to work out how to save what had not yet been lost.

Her own life, of course. But above all, that of her son.

My first date with Catherine was a long time coming, and by the time it did I'd got involved with Wendy. Wendy and I slept together on the first date, a weekday, before we knew a thing

34

about each other. It was exciting, but left us in a peculiar mental place in the morning at her tiny flat, woken by a shrill alarm before six. She exploded from bed with a curse, already late for work and needing me, the relaxed and sleepy home worker, up, dressed and out. She told me off, mildly and quite reasonably, for not retrieving a blood-flecked plaster that had dropped from my knee into the shower tray. From that moment, even as we parted with a quick kiss, we both knew it was already finished. Done for, over.

For a few days afterwards I wondered at the vivid recollection of Wendy's cramped shower stall, the black mould on the ceiling, the flaking emulsion paint on the plastic extractor vent, the torn blue plastic shower curtain with white dolphins on. All those details clung to me more intimately than the fleeting recollection of me piercing her body with mine. Were either of us really present for that? I still don't know. But we'd already lost romantic momentum. I was certain I'd never hear from her again.

When I messaged Catherine again in September, she was already on four date-nights per week. This was a woman who believed in preparation. Years later she showed me some of the copious notes she made about the candidates and their background, learned by heart before each date. The first meeting was always at The Weavers' Tryst, a rambling pub a mile from her house. It was part of a national chain, but had a quiet conservatory bar, and the date was always, at her suggestion, around seven p.m. and for just an hour. The excuse was that she had to go off to babysit her three-year-old niece,

Gayle. That was a lie, but accomplished two objectives. One, it allowed her to slip away early from what she called the Disaster Boys. Despite the screening phone calls, there were no end of DBs: motor-mouths, macho-men, control freaks, know-it-alls and, of course, the dreaded knocker watchers. Two, it allowed her to assess a reaction to the idea of parenthood without having to ask such a car-crash question so early in the dating process. So, before leaving on the imagined babysitting errand, she would show her date a picture of Gayle on her phone. The reactions, from mute repulsion to adoring grin, gave her a useful pointer and saved her a lot of time further down the relationship road.

By the time Catherine tried this on me, in the first week of October, I must already have passed a few tests. I cooed over the child (it wasn't hard, she was adorable), and soon afterwards Catherine checked her phone. 'Oh. Caroline has to stay in now. The babysitting's cancelled.' She smiled at me. 'If you don't have to go, can I buy you another drink?'

With planning and preparation and plenty of time, Catherine had got to where she wanted to be. But now there is no plan, no opportunity to prepare and no time.

She just has to wing it. Survival instinct, nothing more.

Chapter Five

The car is doing 60, twice the speed limit. Fretwell reaches into the pocket of his grey hoodie, smears of dried blood matting the fine, reddish hairs of his wrist, and retrieves a packet of cigarettes. He flicks open the top, presses one to his mouth, and tosses the packet to Cousins. Then he pulls out a lighter, flicks open a flame, and sucks greedily. Catherine notices faint brown marks on the cigarette where he has touched it. I don't mean to be egotistical, but that is my blood, and she knows it. The acrid stench and fog of smoke fills the car. I'm surprised that even I, a persistent spirit due in another place, has been allowed this sense along with all the others.

Ethan stares open-mouthed at the blue-grey miasma, and turns to his mother. He is only one, but he already knows. Catherine abhors smoking, almost more than anything else a person can do. And she has always considered it unforgivable to expose a child to cigarette smoke. I can understand, as no one else could, the level of self-control that Catherine exhibits by saying nothing. It is her job at this stage to be invisible, inaudible, no impediment whatsoever to the will of her captors. It's the one state of being we have in common, though mine is not by choice.

Cousins turns to the driver. 'Where we going, Fretty?'

'Out of here. Don't hassle me. I need to think.' The speedo needle flicks up to 65. Ahead of him there is a big complex junction, with traffic lights on red, two lanes of vehicles in each direction, a right filter. Pedestrian railings, the green lights flashing for those on foot. Fretwell doesn't even pause. He guns down the empty right filter, screeches over into the yellow box, and pulls a tyre-smoking left across the path of the straight-ahead traffic which has just been given green. The turn throws Catherine against the right-hand passenger door. She looks at Ethan, and he is laughing. Mummy play!

She tries to find a smile to flick back, but it's gone wrong: all crinkled wet eyes and jagged open mouth. Catherine knows this road. It leads along an industrial estate, with lots of service roads. It's the back way to the Asda that they were at earlier, in what already seems like a different life.

'We could go to George's garage,' Cousins says.

'Fuck that.'

'Why not?'

'Don't fucking trust him.' Fretwell gets out his phone. It's only a week old, but is greasy and has a cracked screen. The burner phones rarely last. Fretwell likes to throw them. Shoot the messenger, every time. Perhaps too petty to be called a philosophy, it's certainly a habit.

'I'll call him,' Cousins says, eyeing the speedo as it edges over 60 again, Fretwell only glancing up occasionally.

'Fuck off.' Fretwell accelerates, glances down and presses redial. He's calling Blades. He didn't want to, but there's no choice now. He knows he's fucked up, and Blades will be unhappy. No one likes to make Blades unhappy, because there are consequences. But he needs help that only the head of the gang can provide. If he had Cousins do it, that would be loss of prestige. And it would signal fear. Fretwell would never admit to that.

The phone rings out, on and on. He's wondering if he'll have to leave a message and how to phrase it. Then he hears Blades' low voice answering.

'Sparko didn't have it,' Fretwell says. 'Yeah, we put the screws on.' Pause. 'No. We're not in it. We had to leave it. It wouldn't start.' As he lies, his eyes slide sideways to Janile. The thought is easily read. If he let on that Cousins lost the keys, he'll have to explain to Blades. The truth was that the keys to the Vauxhall were somewhere in the stairwell near Lorraine Caldwell's body. Catherine, soaking up every detail she can of her captors, notes a look of complicity reflected in Janile's slight smile of gratitude.

Fretwell listens as Blades lays into him. Catherine can't make out what exactly is being said, but she senses his surprise in the jerky head movements he is making, and his attempts to justify himself. Finally Fretwell moves the phone away from his head and stares at it.

'What's he say?' Cousins asked.

Fretwell doesn't say anything for a moment, but accelerates, racing across a junction on which they should have given way. 'We're on our own.'

'What?'

'He won't lift a finger.' Fretwell smashes the phone into the dashboard, then lets it fall to the floor. 'He won't lift a fucking finger.'

'So where are we going then?'

'Do you expect me to spell it out?' Fretwell glares at him, and then lets his eyes slide towards Catherine. 'Moron.' He knows that Sparko rents a lock-up garage. It's a good place to start looking for the money.

Ahead, an articulated lorry is reversing out into the street. It is halfway across, its reversing beeps goading Fretwell to smash his fists against the steering wheel in frustration, as he is forced to slow. He and Cousins look around frantically, seeking an exit. There are already cars waiting. There's no space to get past. Fretwell bumps the car up onto the pavement, scattering a few pedestrians, and drops down onto a narrow road running parallel. Catherine knows the road. This is the one-way access to the back of Asda, but Fretwell is going the wrong way. He immediately goes nose to nose with a dirty black Warrior 4x4 and, with pedestrian barriers on both sides, is forced to a halt in a cacophony of horns.

'Get out the fucking way you stupid arsehole!' Fretwell bellows.

The Warrior's door opens and a beefy bloke in his forties in paint-stained overalls jumps out. He's swearing and pointing, and waddling towards them in that unhurried don't-mess-with-me walk. This is a guy who is used to doing the intimidating, the kind who stars in YouTube road-rage videos, giving cyclists a hard time. Here, he's bitten off more than he can chew. Way more. Cousins is already sliding out of the door, gun extended in his hand in the gap between door and windscreen.

'You got something to say to me?'

The big guy jumps back, hands raised, and high-tails it behind his own vehicle.

With Cousins back in, Fretwell bangs the Nissan into reverse, puts his arm round the back of the passenger seat and scowls behind him. The crease between his eyebrows is deep with concentration as he looks past Catherine and whines the car backwards at nearly 40 miles an hour. He skilfully follows the sinuous route of the narrow road. A quick U-turn and he's facing the entrance to the Asda car park, trolley bay to one side, disabled parking to the other, and row upon congested row of customer parking, straight ahead.

'Which way?' Fretwell yells to Cousins.

'Jesus man, ain't no idea. I've never been here—'

Catherine speaks. 'You can get out through the service road on the left, round the back of the trolley bay.'

'Oi, didn't I tell you to shut it?' Fretwell says, glaring at her.

'Sorry,' she says.

He turns left into the service road, and demands of her: 'Where's it go?'

'It leads round the back past the service bay,' she says in a small voice. 'If you bump up over the pavement at the end, where the bollards are broken. You're actually behind the petrol forecourt by the main road on the other side.'

Fretwell follows the route, and sure enough after mounting the broken pavement beyond the truck loading bays takes the car through to the car wash area of the Asda fuel forecourt. The main road is nearby, with quick access to the motorway, and Manchester's ring road.

'Fucking hell,' Cousins laughs, finally recognising where they are. 'We using hostage-nav, ain't we?'

'Fuck off.' Fretwell says. He turns to his right and sees a white Transit van at the back of the forecourt. The driver, a turbaned Sikh in a windcheater and jeans, is just walking to the back doors, which are open. He steps inside, and then the metallic scrape of heavy objects being shifted is heard.

'Right. That's our new wheels.' He turns to Catherine, and the shape of his face changes as a realisation comes to him. 'Oi. Giz yer phone. Now.'

Catherine picks up her bag and is just about to root through it when Fretwell snatches the whole thing away from her. He upends it over the handbrake, spilling purse, wet wipes, lipstick, mascara, tampons as well as the phone. He grabs the phone and the purse, and shoves them in the pocket of his bloodstained hoodie.

'Right, we're on,' he says to Cousins. They open the car doors and Fretwell turns to Catherine, putting his face close to her and whispers. 'If you make a fucking sound I shall come back and cut your baby's head right off and shove it back up your c—.'

The vile word he uses horrifies her, but she nods mutely, believing him absolutely. No one would doubt he was capable of doing precisely what he said. As the two men get out of the car, she watches them saunter over the ten yards to the back of the van, as if they were going to greet a mate. Cousins has the gun in the waistband of his jeans. Fretwell's knife isn't visible.

For a moment she has the car to herself, and to Ethan. She looks at our child, his squall now forgotten, playing with Lugs, concentrating on trying to pull off the black embroidered nose with his tiny pale fingers. A blessed moment of normality. The groceries are in the boot, bought less than an hour ago at this very store. My Man City pennant, ripped from the rear-view mirror by Fretwell, lies on the floor. Somewhere above the faint drone of traffic she can hear a cheerful radio voice, a snatch of song she knows. Something by Adele. Radio 2. She closes her eyes, to savour this oasis of calm, and takes a deep breath. But something kicks inside her. She cannot waste this moment of freedom.

She is in the middle seat at the back, wearing a seatbelt that she put on after one particularly wild turn. Now she unclips it. The car keys are not in the ignition, so she can't drive off. She looks around. A rusting shipping container partially shields the car from view of the petrol station forecourt and presumably its CCTV, 30 yards away. Closer to her there is a car wash, marked as out of order. A compressed air station, a pressure washer. Two parked cars. In the other direction, at the back of the Asda store, a young man in overalls has emerged from a loading bay. She watches him, maybe 50 yards away. He cups his hands to light a cigarette: that characteristic hunch, then the lifted head, eyes squinting into the distance, the slow exhalation. The smoker's pleasure. She can feel it in her own lungs. Today is the day she would start smoking, if she could. If it wouldn't affect Ethan.

Everything is different now.

The lad glances in her direction, against the sallow sunlight. He won't be able to see her in the back of the car. But he is staring. He must be wondering whether it's really just red paint all over the front. She thinks about opening the window. It's been ten seconds since her captors went around the back of the van. She can't see or hear them. Just contemplating action makes her throat dry, and her hands tremble. She reaches for the window button, wondering what she could say, and if she could make herself heard.

Then there is a metallic noise, like an avalanche of saucepans. She turns to the Transit, which is rocking gently from side to side. The Sikh is ejected from the back, and rolls on the ground. A slightly rusted fridge-freezer follows and lands on him. His arms twitch, but that is it. The man is later identified as Bikram Singh, 36, married with a young daughter. Another pointless death. Fretwell and Cousins burst from the doors, slam them closed and run to the front of the van, one each side. They jump in and start the engine. The van starts to pull away, and for a moment, just a moment, Catherine feels a surge of relief. A joy that her captors are going away and she and Ethan are safe. The shout of joy stalls in her throat as the van pulls alongside the Nissan. She can hear a siren in the distance now. She turns to look. A police car has turned into the petrol station. Cousins jumps from the van, and pulls open the rear door next to Ethan.

'Out. NOW.'

He springs the belt clip on Ethan's car seat, and tugs the child out by one arm.

'NO, NO!' she screams. 'You can't take him!'

She scrambles over the child seat and Cousins immediately seizes her by the hair. 'Don't worry, sister, we're taking you both,' he growls, passing the crying infant to her. She enfolds Ethan in her arms, his warm cheek against hers, even as a cold gun barrel rests against her temple. 'Come on, MOVE.' He backs her towards the Transit as the police patrol car slews to a halt ten yards away.

A female uniformed officer, short, blonde maybe 30, is out of the passenger door even before it has stopped. The driver's door is thrown open too, and there is yelling from the Transit. 'Nail the bitch' is barely articulated when a deafening sound right by Catherine's ear stuns her, and echoes from the walls of the Asda.

A gunshot.

Later reports would show that PCs Jennifer Hartley and Tessa McDonald were called away from an investigation of criminal damage at Leigh Park School just half a mile away by reports of what seemed to be a robbery and hit and run. Three 999 calls had variously described an apparent robbery of KG Stores in Claremont Road, the knocking down of a cyclist in the adjoining street, Walton Road, who was seen to be clinging to a windscreen, and a few minutes later an attempt to mow down pedestrians near the Hulme Asda a mile or so away. While no one agreed on the make of the car, everyone had noticed the blood on the bonnet.

Jenny Hartley had only been in Greater Manchester Police for four months. She had been a PC in the comparatively calm rural Lancashire town of Oswaldtwistle, but after divorcing the father of her five-year-old daughter a year ago, had transferred to Manchester, city of her birth, where she would have her parents available to babysit. She was on the dating scene again, and enjoying it, and she loved being part of a big busy police force. All she had wanted to do was to be part of something that mattered, where she could make a difference.

With a bit of action too. That's what she had told her dad.

His reply, more prescient than he imagined: careful what you wish for, Jenny.

It was PC Jenny Hartley, drawing on adolescent knowledge of Manchester, who had suggested to McDonald they take the same shortcut through the industrial estate that was known to Catherine. If she had not done so, or had heeded the suggestion over the radio from the DCI to wait for back-up, she would not have found herself in such mortal danger. A little knowledge, she should have known, is a dangerous thing.

Hartley was laden with the full paraphernalia of the modern police officer. Stab vest, equipment belt, radio, torch, CS gas spray, handcuffs, bodycam. McDonald, being more senior and fully trained, had all this plus a Taser. It's normally enough to make an arrest, assuming you can catch your suspect weighed down with that lot. Face to face, the prospect of a Taser shot is enough to make most criminals pause for thought. It's supposedly the most painful thing you will ever feel. So PCs Hartley and McDonald thought they were well-enough prepared to take on a hit-and-run driver.

But this is no hit and run. This is deliberate.

Neither Hartley nor McDonald expect to run into anyone quite as tooled up as Fretwell and Cousins. Nor so desperate.

When Hartley spots the beige Nissan parked behind the petrol station she calls it in to the control room. Other vehicles, she is told, are five minutes away. But when she identifies the lanky figure of Janile Cousins, a man whose mugshot is on every GMP computer, just 20 yards in front of her, she decides that she can't afford to wait. It is only when she is out of the car and running towards him that she realises that the redhead is holding a child, and that she is a hostage rather than an accomplice. Only then does it make sense. The woman's hair held like a noose above her head, her neck stretched, the gun barrel pointing at her skull. Cousins is walking her backwards towards the back of a Transit.

'Don't you fucking MOVE,' Cousins screeches at Hartley, his voice ragged and panicky. 'I'll kill 'em both, right?'

Hartley stops, and raises her hands, but hears movement in the patrol car. Tessa is on the radio. She can hear the control room, the squawk and crackle and she can hear Tessa's voice, low but firm, and a moment later she hears a shout from the driver of the Transit. That is when the patrol car's windscreen seems to explode.

Catherine too hears the yell from the van that precedes the shot, but can hear little for a while afterwards. Cousins is still dragging her away by the hair to the van, and it is all she can do to hold Ethan to her body, to shield him from the mayhem around her.

Some things only became clearer much later. PC Jenny Hartley, arms aloft, expected to be hit by Janile Cousins' shot and flinched at the bang, despite her best intentions. A frosted hole appeared in the windscreen five yards to the right of where she stood.

Fretwell's order, 'Nail the bitch,' had been intended to spur Cousins to shoot Hartley, the only officer he could see. And it was Cousins' intention to comply.

But he missed.

Cousins had never fired the Czech-made CZ-75 pistol before. It was acquired as a replica in Germany, part of a cache of cheap and supposedly neutralised Eastern Bloc weapons bought by Blades for the gang. They were all re-engineered in a workshop near Wageningen in the Netherlands so they would fire, and smuggled into the UK on a car ferry to Hull in 2014. Like a number of the guns, the one that Cousins looked after never fired quite true.

But what no one then knew was that the errant bullet, winging low and to the left, crashing through the windscreen of the squad car, had hit PC Tessa McDonald on the left jaw hinge, breaking it before being deflected upwards by her teeth into her cranium. The massive bleed to the brain would mean she would never regain consciousness. And her attempt to radio in the number plate of the van and the hostage situation was never accomplished.

Catherine and Ethan are chucked into the back of the Transit van at that point, the doors slam closed behind them, and they have nothing but a filthy piece of carpet to lie on. She hears the

48

second and third shots, but doesn't know what has happened until she hears Fretwell's hyena laugh, and sees the brotherly arm around Cousins' shoulder as he climbs into the van's passenger seat. Fretwell joyfully revs the engine and pulls away, bumping across what feels like rough ground. Catherine props herself up, her back to the seats, holding Ethan in one arm, the other grabbing hold of a metal stanchion. The first few seconds of the journey are like a fairground ride, her legs sliding on the carpet, an oil-stained piece of what was once floral stair carpet.

Despite everything that has happened, Ethan still has Lugs with him. The child's tiny fist holds up the limp, stained rabbit to her.

'Lugs,' he says, and offers it to her with a smile.

Ethan still sleeps in our room, in a cot on Catherine's side. Look at him. He's been sleeping right through the night now for six months, but nobody told me to expect the little sounds he makes. The burbling, the sputtering. Ethan manages to blow soft raspberries for minutes at a time, then little snorts. Often there is a movement which I can tell is unhappy, and a little mew of frustration which is often a prelude to a full jag of crying. But quite often he moves, emits a huge and worldly sigh, then sinks back into sleep.

To hear my child, wandering in his own dreams, reaching to the nearest corners of a world he has only just started to explore, fills me with such protective emotions. Just last week, he made his first use of tools. I watched him trying to reach Lugs, who was on the settee, by the cushions at the back, and out of his reach. He tried an exploratory cry, to see if I, as a

49

busy Daddy, would drop my website work, and race over from the dining table to fetch it for him. I didn't. So he crawled over to his plastic toy bus and scooted it towards the sofa. He then tipped the bus on its side, hauled himself up onto the side, and standing up used the nine inches of extra height to haul himself onto the settee.

A child takes in so much more than we can imagine, and learns so much faster than we can appreciate. All the good things; the love, the hugs, the language they soak up at such an incredible rate. The innocence of a baby is manifest in a single concept: their utter trust that the world is a benign place, and that no harm can befall them.

As parents, we go to such lengths to protect them from the bitter and heartbreaking reality.

We feed them the whitest of lies.

But the truth will out. And when it does the protective fabric of childhood starts to fray at the edges. For most children that unravelling is gradual, and manageable. For Ethan, I fear, it is too abrupt, too much of a shock. I cannot see that far into the future, but I fear for him.

The van is gone. PC Jenny Hartley finds she is lying sideways on a patch of gravel, with something warm trickling into her eye. Blood. The side of her face is pressed into the unforgiving though surprisingly warm surface. She has never looked closely at gravel before, and just here it is salted with a myriad interesting objects. Glittering crystals of car glass, flattened cigarette ends, scraps of greying miscellaneous polythene.

Further off is a crushed water bottle, a fruit juice box with drinking straw, a magenta drop still sparkling within it, catching the watery sun. Ribena, she realises. And a child's dummy. This last is too grimy, surely, to have been in the mouth of the young hostage. This one has the filth of years, its brown rubber nipple split.

The crackle of her police radio breaks into her reverie. She tries to move an arm, but cannot seem to reach the device at her chest. She hears the sound of hurried footsteps approaching. 'Jesus Christ,' says a young man she cannot yet see. 'Oh Jesus.'

'Is she alive?' shouts an older out of breath male voice, also behind her.

'Not by much, I shouldn't think,' says the first.

PC Hartley is determined to speak, at least to contest that opinion, but can only wheeze out sighs where words should be.

'What'd she say?' says the older man.

She then tries to tilt her hips to move onto her back and see these gallant knights, her rescuers. That is when the pain, which had so far been crouching within her, biding its time, shrieks its arrival.

'Ah, hurts,' she gasps.

'Keep still love,' the older one says, coming into view and crouching down beside her. 'We've called the ambulance. It's on its way.' He reaches out a hairy hand with a silver wristwatch on it and grasps hers, tightly. The hand is warm, comforting, and a lifeline. It pushes back some of the pain. She tries a smile, but from the reaction of the man, she thinks it must have come out wrong. It's pity that comes back from him. Pity.

PC Jenny Hartley was shot twice. The first bullet creased her scalp and bled profusely across her face and neck, but was never a danger to her life. The second hit her torch where it was clipped to her stab vest, shattering it and winding her. The real damage, which neither of her initial helpers recognised, was being run over by the van. Liam Fretwell's cruel action shattered both her tibia, one fibula and a bone called the talar on top of her left foot. She had never heard of the talar, but the damage to it would cause her to walk with a limp for the rest of her life. But at least she was alive.

Unlike PC Tessa McDonald. Unlike Sparko Sinclair and Lorraine Caldwell. Unlike the Sikh van driver.

Unlike me.

Chapter Six

Catherine now has no idea where they are going or what is going to happen to her and Ethan. They are hostages to a cause which has no clear objective and as far as she can see can only end in disaster. She looks around the inside of the van, her metal box of captivity. There are no handles on the inside of the doors, no way she can escape, even if the vehicle stops for a junction or traffic lights. There are no weapons, either. Two hook-ended bungee cords, stretched across a ceiling panel, and some flattened and dirty cardboard boxes are all the resources she can look to. Besides, with Ethan in her arms, what chance does she have? The two men who control her destiny are young, impulsive and totally cold-blooded. All she can hope to do is to make herself useful, to help them achieve their objective to get away. To get them to extend to her just a little trust. To buy time, and perhaps mercy.

Ethan, who she had held tight to her chest, is grizzling a little. He's been remarkably calm so far, but this is bound to change. He may only be a year old, but he knows his routine. He's due a sleep. His nappy needs to be changed, she can smell it already. Soon he will be getting hungry. She's increasingly nervous that if he really starts to cry, she won't have any of the resources to make him stop.

'We've fucking done it now, Fretty. Dead cops.'

'Stop being an old woman. We've got fucking sprog insurance,' he said, indicating Ethan with a thumb. 'Fully comp, mate. We're bulletproof.'

'We should dump 'em, make a run for it,' Cousins says, shaking his head.

'No way.' Fretwell permits himself a glance over his shoulder. Catherine looks up and catches his eye.

'What the fuck are you looking at, bitch?'

She doesn't reply, but averts her gaze.

'Oi! Answer when I speak to you. If I have to come back there you'll fucking regret it.'

'Sorry.' Her reply is a hoarse whisper, her hands shaking.

Fretwell turns away, a sly smile of victory on his face. 'Fucking women. Only useful for one thing,' he says to Cousins.

'Fat bitch be no good even for that,' Cousins chuckles.

To Catherine, the insult is a relief. It cuts just one thread from the braid of fear that is bound around her heart. Ethan is beginning to wriggle, and she cannot long delay what she knows will be coming. She shushes him, as softly and gently as she can, swinging him in the crook of her free arm, which is now aching from the long minutes of holding him. She lets go of the stanchion, lifts her fleece, unbuttons her blouse and lifts Ethan to her nipple. With her back now to the rear of the seat, they cannot easily see what she is doing. The feeling of the soft mouth on her breast, the slight rub of Ethan's few teeth, gives her some comfort.

'Fuck.' Fretwell glances in the wing mirror, and now switches his concentration to the road. The van is heading into the centre of the city on the A56, with Manchester United's Old Trafford Stadium on his left. A police patrol car, one of the motorway pursuit BMWs, is approaching fast on the overtaking lane. The chequered blues and yellows and the roof mounting give it away even though the lights aren't on. The next traffic light junction offers a left turning he knows well. Sir Matt Busby Way, the road that goes to the East Stand of the stadium, a street he walked with his father many times as a boy, going to see United play.

The lights are red, and he slows the van down as he eases into the left-hand lane, opposite a Subway sandwich shop. They are in a queue of a dozen vehicles.

'Could do with a sarnie,' Cousins says, staring at the shop.

'You'll have to fucking wait.' Fretwell watches the patrol car ease up next to him. 'We got company.' The officer in the passenger seat looks up at him. He is a middle-aged guy with specs and short grey hair. Fretwell can't help himself. He stares back, the sullen stony glare that is his default shop window to the rest of humanity.

'Don't stare him out, Fretty, for fuck's sake,' Cousins says. 'Attracts attention.' He turns around to look down at Catherine. He points a warning finger at her. 'Keep quiet.' His eyes slide down to her partially exposed breast. She doesn't want to risk eye contact, but she is somehow aware of a softening of his gaze, and a movement in his mouth. She would like to believe that this is a skein of empathy, even paternal feelings, but something tells her it could be the stirrings of something awful. Very slowly, she moves her arm to obscure his view. His dead eyes climb to her face, and as she glances at him his slight smile tells her she was right to worry. A worm of fear wriggles slowly through her entrails. She can hardly believe that she might find Fretwell, for all his violence, an ally against Cousins' sinister predatory interests.

The lights go green, and Fretwell takes the turn calmly. The patrol car heads straight on.

'Lost the bastard,' he chuckles.

The relief doesn't last long. Ahead, where the road leads into the pedestrian plaza and a huge car park, the road is lined with police riot vans under the shadow of Old Trafford. Dozens of them, with their window grilles in place. Fretwell swears softly.

'Fretty, turn around,' Cousins says, pointing. 'Look at all them pigs.'

'I can see 'em. Do you think I'm fucking blind?'

'There's hundreds of 'em, man!'

'Shut it, stop being an old woman.'

Dozens of cops in black overalls and helmets lean against the side of the vehicles, drinking from polystyrene cups and chatting. As the Transit slows to pass the first of them, the cops stare. This time Fretwell keeps his eyes straight ahead, his knuckles white on the wheel, making the four tattooed letters of the rudest word in English stand out on his knuckles.

'They'll have the van's number, won't they?' Cousins asks.

'Piss off. They're not looking for us, not yet. Too soon. This is something else.'

Catherine had heard on the traffic reports that morning that a large scale anti-terror exercise would cause congestion in central Manchester later in the day. That information might be useful to lower her captors' stress levels, but every time she speaks seems like playing Russian roulette. She stays quiet, moving Lugs from side to side to amuse Ethan.

Fretwell takes a left into a quieter suburban road.

'But as soon as they trace the turban guy, they'll look for his van,' Cousins says.

'By then we'll be safe.'

'So what are we gonna do with them?' Cousins jerks a thumb over his shoulder.

Catherine looks up. She knew she has to build on what Cousins has said. It is very dangerous, very high-risk, but it has to be done. 'If you release us, I'll not say a word. I promise,' she says quietly.

'Yeah, right,' Fretwell says. 'You know too much already.'

Ethan has been angelic for the last 15 minutes, but finally it all becomes too much. He takes a big shuddering intake of breath, his mouth stretches wide and he bawls. Inside the Transit van the squall echoes from metal panels, intensifying the sound, which pierces like a circular saw. Catherine embraces him as tightly as she dares, the back of his soft hair, the gentle eggshell skull so delicate in her hands.

'I told you, shut him up!' Fretwell bellows, banging his hand on the wheel.

'I'm trying, but I don't think I can keep him quiet any more. His nappy needs changing.'

'I thought there was a stink,' Cousins mutters.

'If I can't get him changed he'll cry. I won't be able to stop him,' she says.

'For fuck's sake!' Fretwell jams the brakes on, slows the van to a halt, then leans over the back of the seat. He stares at Ethan as if the power of his eyes alone could force him into silence. 'I think we've heard enough from you about what your fucking baby needs. You'll do what you're fucking told and you'll do it straightaway, all right?' He waves the knife towards her. There is dried blood all over it.

My blood. And that of the Sikh.

Catherine tries to staunch her tears, which are joining those of Ethan. 'I'm trying to help you,' she whispers. 'If I can change his nappy and get him to sleep, he'll be quiet. If he's crying in here, it will attract attention.'

'Don't I fucking know it!' Fretwell bellows. He pulls up at a T-junction that takes them back on the A56. 'The filth will already have this number plate, so the sooner I get it off the road the better.' He pulls out, and turns left towards central Manchester.

The van is now travelling at speed, and Fretwell and Cousins are both kept busy trying to spot police patrol cars. Two pass in the other direction in five minutes. Ethan is now in a disgusting condition, the stench so bad that the captors fully lower both windows.

'All right,' says Fretwell, to Catherine. 'I can't fucking stand this no more. There's a chemist here and Jazz will get you what you need.' He pulls up alongside a parade of shops.

'Will I, fuck,' Cousins says, his eyes stabbing towards Fretwell.

'Give him some cash,' Fretwell says to Catherine.

'But you've got my purse,' she say.

'So? That's mine now,' Fretwell smirks. 'So you got any more?'

Catherine suppresses a sigh, and feels in the pocket of her fleece. Sometimes she does have a note or a few coins there. All she finds is 40 pence, a chapstick and a tissue. 'Just give me ten pounds back. I'll get it, no one is expecting to see me.'

Fretwell laughs, and shakes his head.

'You should get it, Fretty,' says Cousins.

'I'm not paying for it, and I'm driving, ain't I?'

'Well, I ain't getting it,' Cousins says.

'The van fucking stinks, Jazz.'

Catherine senses an opportunity. She pinches Ethan on the underside of the leg, where no one can see her, and he immediately gulps and then starts to wail.

'Get 'em out of here for Christ's sake,' Cousins says.

'And what do we bargain with when the filth arrive?' Fretwell asks, raising his voice above the sound of Ethan's sobs.

'Ditch 'em.'

Fretwell turns to Catherine and says: 'Just nappies, right?'

Cousins laughs, and shakes his head. 'Fucking hell, man. You'll be doing the ironing next.'

The explosion of violence that follows is over in less than a second. Fretwell has his hand wrapped in Cousins' hair, the head bent back over the seat, the five-inch blade of the knife indenting his long exposed throat.

'What did you say, bruv?' Fretwell whispers.

Cousins' Adam's apple rises and falls slowly, his breath shallow. 'Nothing, Fretty. I never meant nothing by it.'

'Right. You're fucking getting what she needs.' Fretwell turns to her. 'Tell him.'

Catherine knows that everything she needs is in the baby change bag in the abandoned Nissan: nappies, baby wipes, antiseptic gel, a changing pad, muslin squares. She can't begin to ask for all that. The bottomless rage that animates Fretwell should not be provoked. Then there is another matter.

'Can I say something?' Catherine asks meekly.

'Christ, what the fuck is it now?' he sighs.

'You're both covered in blood,' Catherine said. 'You'll be noticed.'

'She's right Fretty, I'm splattered,' Cousins says.

'So? You could have cut yourself.'

'A blood-soaked man, asking for nappies...' Catherine knows that Fretwell understands what she is saying.

'Right.' Fretwell squints out towards the chemist's shop, and then turns his gaze back to Catherine. 'You've got one minute, right? Get what you need and get back here. I'll be watching.'

'Thank you.' Catherine stands up with Ethan in her arms, ready to walk to the rear of the van.

'Oi, leave him here,' Fretwell says, pointing to the floor.

'No, no I can't leave him.' Fresh tears well up in Catherine's eyes as she strokes the child's head.

'Obviously, you stupid bitch, I'm not letting you both out, am I? Jazz, take the kid, I'll let her out.'

'I'm not holding it. It stinks. Leave it on the floor.'

Catherine doesn't move, her eyes switching from one captor to the other. Cousins points the gun at her. 'Heard what I said, didn't ya?'

She kisses Ethan and kneels on the filthy carpet. 'Be brave for me little man, I'll just be a minute. Be quiet and I'll be back in no time,' she coos, her voice wavering. But almost immediately the child begins to cry. Fretwell gets out and walks round to the rear of the van. He opens the door, and lets her out. For the first time in half an hour she is in the outside world. But without Ethan in her arms she feels bereft.

Fretwell leans in to her ear. 'Listen to me,' he says. 'I can see everything you do in there. Grab the stuff and get out. You say a word to anyone I'll slice the kid's head off, understand?'

She nods her head mutely. Ethan's plaintive sobbing can be heard quite clearly. Her heart feels like it is being torn in two. Fretwell sits in the rear doorway, the door half closed so passing traffic cannot see him, but giving him a good view of the chemist's shop. He lifts up his wrist, glances at his watch and says: 'Your minute starts now.'

Catherine sprints the 20 yards to the shop, a small self-service store, with a white-coated Asian-looking pharmacist in view. As she bursts through the door she sees two elderly women waiting at the only till. She finds a big package of nappies easily, but dislodges a cascade of jars as she reaches for the baby wipes. She feels everyone staring, as if she were some drunk on a rampage. Her watch shows her time half gone, and she feels like she is carrying a sign that says shoplifter. She radiates guilt for what she is about to do. Indeed, the shop staff already seem to know what is about to happen. A bespectacled male shop assistant, Asian, skinny and perhaps 16 is between her and the exit. The man in the white coat, perhaps his father, has emerged from behind the counter and a middle-aged woman already has the phone in her hand.

There is no time for subtlety.

Catherine charges for the door. As the lad attempts to grab the package of Pampers, she elbows him hard in the face, and he tumbles backwards into the window display. She bashes the door with her shoulder and then sprints back to the van. Fretwell opens the back door wide, a huge grin on his face, pushes her in and slams the door behind her. He then jumps into the driver's seat, guns the engine and races away. Catherine has barely reached Ethan by the time the van takes the first corner, but the child's distress is quickly eased by her presence.

'Did you see that, Jazz? Smacked him down in one go. I'm well impressed.'

'Yeah. Should have got her to get some fags,' Cousins says. 'Left mine in the other car.'

'So you're a well experienced fucking shoplifter now, eh?' Fretwell asks her.

'You left me no choice,' she says. It is Catherine's first act of violence since the age of 13, when she slapped Nicola Brown for calling her carrot top. Now, back safely with Ethan, she has the luxury to indulge the waves of shame she feels.

'What's your name then?' A little ray of admiration has lightened Fretwell up a little. Maybe there is honour amongst thieves.

She is prepared to take a risk, to assert herself. 'I'm Catherine Blake,' she said. 'And you've killed my husband.'

'Life's tough, bitch,' Cousins says. 'He shouldn't have tried to block the car.'

'It was an act of bravery, to save my life and our son.'

'It was an act of fucking stupidity,' Fretwell laughs, as he accelerates, bashing up through the gears for emphasis.

'A supreme act of love…' Catherine feels good to be able to say it.

'Now you'll have a criminal record an all,' Cousins chuckles.

'Can you stop somewhere so I can change him?' she asks.

'Christ almighty,' Fretwell says. 'Just do it, you stupid bitch.'

Catherine kneels on the carpet, bracing her knees as wide apart on the carpet as she can, her head braced against the back of the Transit seats so she has both hands free for the task. She undoes the poppers on his baby suit, and unclips the safety pin on his terry nappy. She can already see that it is going to be bad, and when she releases it the smell is appalling. She had always tried to be environmentally conscious, and doesn't like using disposables, but this is an emergency. She folds the fouled nappy and bundles it into the disposal bag, which she ties tightly. Her captors complain bitterly about the stench.

She hasn't had time to get cream or antiseptic gel, but at least she has a good supply of baby wipes. She needs them. Ethan is badly chapped, no wonder he has been crying so much. She cleans quickly and efficiently, squeezes him into a fresh nappy and wipes her hands as carefully as she can. 'All done,' she says.

'Thank Christ for that,' Fretwell says. 'I'm suffocating.'

Cousins looks at him, and asks: 'How long before we are there?'

'Ten minutes,' he replies. 'Then we can be shot of them, one way or the other.'

But it isn't to be. Developments elsewhere are destined to tighten the screw on all four.

'We gotta dump the van,' says Cousins. 'Them at the pharmacy may have got the number, right?'

Fretwell shrugs. 'When we're ready. A white van blends right in.'

'Excuse me, can I just suggest something?' Catherine says. Fretwell glares at her in the mirror, but she continues: 'You really need some fresh clothes, something with no bloodstains on.'

'So are you going to fucking wash them for us then?' Fretwell spat.

'There's loads of charity shops round here. Give me five minutes and I could get you a hoodie each and a pair of jogging bottoms.'

'Why the fuck would you do that for us, eh?' Fretwell gives her a stony stare.

'Oh believe me, I would be delighted if you both just slipped away undetected.' She looks at Ethan, strokes his hair and leaves unsaid how much she fears the alternative: a nasty, messy and violent end to their captivity.

Cousins slides his eyes sideways to assess Fretwell's reaction.

He knows there is logic in what the woman says. But trusting her for one minute is a lot different than trusting her for five. That same consideration soon bubbles up in Fretwell too.

'Nah, you'd just grass us up, wouldn't ya?' he says, sharing a smirk with Cousins.

'Why would I risk that when you have my precious child here in the van?' she says vehemently. 'If you are to get away, you have to stop drawing attention to yourselves. That means not only fresh clothes, but paying for them properly.'

'Hey, the bitch just wants to do a bit of shopping,' Cousins smirks.

Fretwell drives on for a few minutes, not saying anything. He turns into a side road, and stares out of the window at a row of three charity shops. None are national names, but they clearly have large amounts of stock judging from the bulging rails pressed tight against the front windows. Fretwell stops the van, picks up Catherine's purse from the door pocket and extracts a £20 note.

'Right, there you go. You can buy us something nice for how good we treated you, right? You say a word, and what will happen?' He looks meaningfully at Ethan.

Catherine follows his eyes.

'Say a word and what will happen?' he repeats, emphatically.

'You will murder my child,' she whispers.

'Say it again to remind you,' Fretwell says.

'If I say a word...' Catherine gulps.

'To anyone...' Fretwell reminds her, now bringing out the knife. 'Again!'

'If I say a word to anyone, you will murder my child.' Forced to rehearse the threat, Catherine feels tears roll down her face, and her hands start to shake. 'You've made me all frightened again now,' she says, wiping her sleeve across her eyes.

'That's the exact fucking idea,' Fretwell says. 'Now, take a deep breath, blow that snot out yer nose and get ready to do what you have to do for us. Three minutes, no more.' He passes across the cash, eases open the driver's door, makes his way around to the back of the van and unlocks the rear door.

'I need more time!' Catherine says, as the door opens.

'Nah, keep you focused.'

Catherine hurries off, trying not to run, while Fretwell sits in the back of the van, watching her. She goes into the middle shop, which is a chaotic mix of unsorted clothing. A squat woman with dyed black hair and hoop earrings is behind the counter, reading a magazine. She only glances up briefly.

'Couple of large men's hoodies,' Catherine says.

'That box,' she says indicating a waist high cardboard box. 'Have a look. Everything in there is just two quid.' She turns back to the magazine.

Panic rising up through her chest, Catherine rapidly scans the rest of the shop. Women's clothing, women's shoes. Junk. She turns to the box, and reaches right to the bottom to pull everything out. She immediately finds one light grey hoodie but which might be a bit small. She puts it aside as she searches through the rest. There is a Liverpool FC shirt, paint stained but easily large enough. Now she needs at least one pair of trousers. There seem to be none there.

'Jogging trousers?' She calls out to the woman. She has less than a minute to go.

'Sweatpants on that rail,' she indicates with a casual thumb over her shoulder. 'A pound-fifty.'

Desperate now, Catherine wades to the indicated rail, grabs five of the largest pairs and drops the £20 on the counter. She's already hurrying out when the woman slaps the note on the counter and says, 'I can't change *that*.'

She is back at the van with five seconds to spare, with one hoodie, one football shirt and a stack of joggers in her arms.

Cousins riffles through the clothes and bursts out laughing. He holds up the Liverpool shirt to Fretwell, for all the world like a taunting matador. She doesn't even see the blow which knocks her sideways and bangs her head painfully on a stanchion. She only just manages to avoid falling on Ethan, who is already wailing.

'Are you taking the piss, eh?' Fretwell says, seizing a handful of Catherine's hair. 'Fucking Liverpool!'

'I'm sorry, I'm sorry. It was all they had,' she pleads.

'He hates Liverpool,' Cousins says with glee. 'Still, least it wasn't Man City.'

She scoops the bawling Ethan into her arms, while Fretwell continues to complain to the world in general about the stupidity of women and this one in particular. 'No one in here is going to wear that,' he says.

Cousins has meanwhile squeezed himself into the grey hoodie and a pair of very baggy black jogging bottoms. Fretwell changes into joggers too, but tosses the rest of the clothing aside.

PCs Michael Evans and Daryl Collins are on the M60 Manchester ring road to follow up reports of a break-in at Wardley Business Park when they are alerted to what in typical police understatement is called a serious incident outside an Asda store near Moss Side. They immediately divert to the more urgent case, Evans driving their BMW patrol vehicle off at Junction 12, on the M602 heading east. Before they arrive the control room alerts them to a white Transit van sought in connection with the incident. 'Reports of two hostages taken by two suspects. Passenger in the van believed to be one Janile Cousins, armed and dangerous, and the driver may be Liam Fretwell, on the run from HMP Wakefield. Vehicle last reported on ANPR at 16.32 hours heading north on Trafford Road.' While Evans drives, Collins calls in their position and takes down the number plate details.

Over the radio more reports begin to be made. There is now a link between the incident at Asda, in which at least one police officer is reported to have been critically injured, and the road rage incident an hour ago in Moss Side, which led to one death. Separately a report of shoplifting has just been made by a store on the Eccles New Road in Salford. 'Suspect, female, made her escape in a white van, reported registration number matching stolen vehicle.'

PC Collins, a thick-set and balding officer, nine years in the Greater Manchester force, acknowledges the call handler's report. He double-checks the status of the twin dashboard-and-rear window mounted ANPR cameras. There are no end of white vans in the traffic, but this device can cope with any number of them, behind or in front, two lanes simultaneously, at up to 50 metres, and remotely compares all registration numbers with vehicles of interest listed on the Police National Computer. PC Michael Evans, aged 35, has only last week finished a refresher course on pursuit driving. He is disappointed that in the last five years since he first qualified, chase policy has been toned down because of a spate of lethal accidents involving 'boy racers' while being pursued. The instruction now is to follow but not to attempt to apprehend.

It is while the two officers are turning in to Eccles New Road that the dashboard display flags up a number plate match on a vehicle which just passed in the opposite direction. Evans says that he has just glimpsed a van. Blue lights activated, they pull a hard right turn and then set off back into central Manchester. Before they even spot the van, the control room updates the previous report on the incident outside Asda. 'Confirming one officer dead at the scene, another critical with multiple injuries including gunshot wounds. All firearms units in the area are being called in. Unarmed officers are warned not to approach.'

The chase is on.

It is Fretwell who sees the approaching police BMW in the Transit's big wing mirrors. 'It's the bloody filth again,' he says. The road is busy, a single lane of traffic in each direction, and the patrol car is coming down the middle, sirens wailing, forcing traffic to give way. It is still several hundred yards behind them.

'There's a multi-storey off right,' Cousins says.

'Good. We can dump this thing. And them,' Fretwell says, looking over his shoulder at Catherine and Ethan. He wheels right and takes a slip road which slopes down to the basement entry of an ugly 1960s concrete car park. They lose sight of the police patrol car. It doesn't appear to be following them. Fretwell winds down the window as they approach the ticket machine, grabs a ticket and waits as the barrier lifts. Entering the Stygian gloom, he powers the van gradually up each ramp from one dingy split-level floor to the next. The first two are pretty full, but by the third there are plenty of gaps.

On each ramp, Catherine has to grab hold of the stanchion to stop herself sliding down to the back of the van. The vehicle comes to a halt, and Fretwell and Cousins look out from the fourth floor, one below the open top. It is one of only three vehicles parked here.

'I know this place,' Cousins says. 'There's a walkway to the shopping centre. One floor down, I reckon.'

Fretwell climbs out of the van and leans over the concrete balustrade and squints down over the entrance to the car park that they have just taken. He absorbs the familiar yellow and blue chequer pattern of a Greater Manchester police patrol vehicle, slewed across the exit to the car park. There is no way they can drive out. He swears softly.

Cousins leans over too, gun in hand. 'Let just one of them show me his head.'

'Let's get the fuck out of here anyway,' Fretwell says. He then turns to Catherine and says, 'You stay here five minutes. Don't let me come back and find you out the van.'

Catherine nods and, cradling Ethan, shrinks into the corner of her metal cell. She is more than happy to stay out of the way.

Fretwell and Cousins sprint for the door to the stairwell. They pull it open and enter the besmirched concrete cavity, their two-at-at-time descent creating a slapping echo. The crackle of a police radio drifts up from far beneath. Cousins leans down over the metal railings hoping to spot a uniform to aim at. They hear several sets of heavy footsteps ascending, and the nearby sound of sirens.

'Just down one floor, right?' Fretwell hisses, as he leaps down to the next landing.

'Think so.' Cousins is keeping pace, his pistol in hand.

But the floor beneath has only a blank wall where a door should be. And now resounding in the blank chamber of the staircase is a rhythmic, pulsating noise. A helicopter, approaching fast.

A man's voice booms up the stairs. 'Armed Police. Drop your weapons. You cannot escape. We have blocked off the exits.'

Fretwell and Cousins glance at each other and race back up the stairs, towards the van.

The first Catherine knows is after two minutes of blissful isolation, her captors have returned. 'Jazz, in the back with them,' says Fretwell. Cousins complies, slithering over the seat until he is sitting opposite Catherine, his gun pointing at her.

Things have just turned a whole lot uglier.

Chapter Seven

Patrick Hamilton is out in his prized garden in the pleasant Cheshire village of Prestbury, strimming a patch of nettles blighting his veg patch, when the call comes. His wife Caroline runs out into the garden, phone in hand, to attract his attention, and gets him to turn off the machine. The first he sees is Caroline moving into his line of vision, in pinny and slippers, with flour up to her elbows. 'I think you are needed,' she says. 'It sounds quite urgent.'

Hamilton is a specialist siege negotiator. A former Royal Marine commando, reaching the rank of captain, earning a distinguished service order in the battle of Goose Green on the Falkland Islands in 1983 at the age of 23. Now approaching 60, he is a big bluff man, with a ready smile, an easy laugh and a soft Scottish accent. His ability to win over even the most recalcitrant hostage takers was well established during his time working in Africa for U.S. security outfit Blackwater, when he persuaded an Islamist group in Kenya to release three Dutch holidaymakers. Returning to Britain in 2007, he started to get some work for police forces across the north of England, gaining a Red Centre designation. One of his principal advantages is that he has never been a policeman. That allows him to say that he is a genuine go-between, not someone simply probing for more intelligence. That deflects the hatred so often aimed at the police.

When he picks up the phone in the lounge, showering fragments of weed onto Caroline's recently vacuumed carpet, he hears the voice of Chief Superintendent Neil Fynn, a veteran incident commander in Greater Manchester Police, with whom he has worked on several occasions.

'Paddy, we need you ASAP in central Manchester. We've got a developing siege situation in a multi-storey car park. We have a car on its way to you, but we'll save some time if it can pick you up in Wilmslow.'

'I'll be there in 20 minutes. Get them to meet me outside the Red Lion, I'll be in a black Range Rover.'

'Good. I've got your number, I'll brief you on the way in.'

Fynn is as good as his word, and the phone rings in the car before he is out of the village.

'So what have we got, Neil?' Hamilton asks on the hands-free.

'Two members of the Moss Side Mafia are holding a female and her baby hostage in the back of a Transit van.'

'Armed?'

'Yes. At least one handgun, plus a knife, and they're not afraid to use them. They have already killed at least four, including a female PC. Another female officer is seriously injured.'

'Has contact been made? Are there any demands?'

'No telephone contact as yet. We are building an armed presence in the vicinity, but not ready to put our heads above the parapet. We've emailed you full details of the two suspects.'

The Wilmslow rendezvous made, Hamilton sits in the back of the police Astra studying his phone as the taciturn female driver blue-lights it through rural Cheshire's rush-hour traffic. At this time of day most vehicles are leaving Manchester, so are coming in the opposite direction. There is plenty of space for her ambitious overtaking at up to 80 miles an hour, which sees them at the incident within the hour.

Hamilton knows a key variable in any siege is the character and temperament of the hostage. He has her name and a few basic details. Catherine Blake, 41, an educational administrator. She has just lost her husband to these two, and still has a child to save. One of his priorities is to get to talk to her.

As Hamilton absorbs the details of Fretwell and Cousins' criminal records, and the little sketchy family information available, he realises that these two are likely to be particularly desperate. They are already looking at a long time behind bars for what they have done in just the last hour and a half. With the killing of a female police officer, a whole life tariff is already a possibility, particularly for Fretwell, the older of the two.

Potentially very nasty. There is no particular incentive for these two criminals to leave their hostages alive.

Despite the rhythmic thudding of rotor blades, Ethan is asleep in Catherine's arms. She once again is staring down the barrel of the gun. Janile Cousins is opposite her, his back leaning against one side of the van, hers the other. His long legs are splayed wide in front of him, a proprietorial seizing of space that she read about in the *Guardian*. It is called 'manspreading,' and usually applies to public transport. She has the choice of leaving her outstretched legs where they are, almost touching his, or she could do what women on the bus or the tube normally do and just restrict her space to make way for him. A part of her, the fearful anxious mother, does indeed want to roll into the tiniest most insignificant ball where she cannot be seen. But a bigger part of her, an angry, strident and in recent years assertive strand of her personality says: *why the hell should I?* So she leaves her legs where they are, subtly contesting with her captor the ownership rights in the metal cage they now share.

She can see the soles of his white Nike trainers: wet dirt, dried blood and a grey wad of chewing gum. The laces are undone, one of them blood-soaked. She wonders why he risks tripping up for the sake of fashion.

'What's going on Fretty?' Cousins asks.

'There are cops out there, loads of them. Can't you hear the bastards?'

'No mate, all I can hear is the fucking chopper.'

'They'll have shooters by now,' Fretwell says. He bobs his head quickly out of the open driver's side window, and then peers out of the passenger side too. 'They'll not get us, not while we've got these two. Isn't that right?' he says to her.

'But do they know I am here? Do they know about Ethan?'

'That cop by the Asda saw well enough,' Fretwell says, lighting another cigarette.

'And them at the chemists,' Cousins adds, holding out his arm for a fag. Fretwell glances into the pack, sees there are only three left and puts it back in his pocket. Cousins rolls his eyes and for a moment shares a conspiratorial glance with Catherine. She risks a small smile of acknowledgement.

'If you make sure they know we're here they won't come charging in, will they?' she asks. 'We'll all be safer.'

'Keep your fucking gob shut, all right?' Fretwell dips in his pocket and pulls out a battered smartphone, one she's not seen before. He leans over the seat, and takes a picture of Catherine and Ethan. She is alarmed by this, having no idea what he is up to. Fretwell works away with furrowed brows, and fast fingers. He finishes with a final flourish and looks up, clearly pleased with himself.

'Right. Now you're on Facebook. I've told them that we want that chopper to land on the roof here, to take us out of here in 15 minutes, or we execute you both.'

Catherine can't suppress the whimper that slides through her teeth. She is trembling all over. Ethan looks up at her, offering her Lugs to play with. She takes the battered rabbit, and waggles it back and forth in front of the child's face. She tries to hide her own tears, now coursing down her cheeks, by quietly humming the only tune she can think of: 'The Wheels on the Bus Go Round and Round'.

'Did you ask for some food?' Cousins says. 'I'm starving.'

Fretwell ignores him.

'Are you friends with the police on Facebook?' Catherine asks tentatively.

'Course I'm not, you stupid bitch. But we know they monitor the gang. We got all our music videos on there. It's our shop window. Course, all the deals are on WhatsApp, where the filth can't read them,' he smirks. He pulls a phone from his pocket, and turns it on. It rings immediately and Catherine recognises it as hers.

The familiar ringtone tugs at her heart, and she blinks away tears. 'Can I answer it please? It's probably my mum worried sick about me and Ethan.'

Fretwell ignores her, and stares at the screen for a good half minute before turning it off. A moment later there is different ring tone and Fretwell pulls out the battered phone. He stares at the screen and exchanges a wary glance with Cousins.

'Is it Blades?' Cousins asks.

Fretwell shook his head slowly. 'I think it's the filth.' He continues to watch as it rings.

Catherine wills him to answer. After being tense for so long, her entire body is on the point of overload. Her trembling has turned into visible shaking. She is frightened for herself, but even more for Ethan. She has to keep her wits about her, but she is so tired, so disorientated. If only it would all stop.

The phone stops ringing.

Fretwell looks up and straight out of the windscreen at a block of flats opposite. The thin April light has faded and in the flickering strip lights of the car park the cloudy sky is the colour of a bruise. 'Shit. There's a bloody pig on the roof with a rifle and scope.'

Cousins stands up, and strains forward to look over the seat. 'I can't see him.' The movement causes the van to rock a little.

For just a moment, neither of them is looking at Catherine. The gun, still in Cousins' hand, is pointing at the floor. The weapon is less than two feet away from her own free right hand. She licks her lips as she works up the courage to try grab the pistol. Her breathing becomes ragged as she realises that this is the best chance she has had so far. But then a quick glance down at Ethan makes her realise that even a perfect chance like this does not offer the guaranteed odds she needs to keep her baby safe. And in that moment Cousins moves and the opportunity vanishes.

Catherine silently curses herself for her indecision, but at the same time realises that even with as little as ten minutes to live, she is not ready to take chances with Ethan's life.

'He's hiding behind the air con unit. Give us the shooter.' Fretwell clicks his fingers.

Cousins seems reluctant but after a few seconds passes the weapon, handle first. Fretwell takes it and leans out of the driver's window. The discharge of the weapon and the boom as the shot echoes around the car park wakes Ethan, who begins to wail, piercingly shrill and unignorable .

'Shut it up, for fuck's sake,' Fretwell bellows, as he pulls his head back in.

Cousins kneels behind the seats, scanning the rooftops opposite. 'Did you get him?'

'Nah. Too far away. But I made him think. Hey Jazz, how much ammo you got?'

'Half a boxful, maybe forty, fifty rounds.'

'Right.' Fretwell leans out of the passenger window, aims the weapon, and blows out the car park's strip light. 'Better if they can't see us so well,' he says.

Catherine shushes Ethan, stroking his hair and jiggling him from side to side, but it isn't surprising that the child is so terrified of these deafening bangs.

'For fuck's sake, what's wrong with the little bastard now?' Fretwell asks. Catherine offers only a small smile of contrition and apology. Fretwell doesn't pursue the matter, but returns to his mobile, tapping away for a minute and then finishing with a flourish. 'Right, I sent them a message on Twitter. They're bound to see that.'

What Fretwell and Cousins don't see is the growling arrival in clouds of diesel exhaust of two battleship-grey armoured Land Rover Defenders, one of which is directed in to the ground floor of the car park, while the other waits outside. These two specialist vehicles, bristling with high-technology equipment, carry Greater Manchester Police's Tactical Firearms Unit. Together with four arriving on the car park roof by helicopter, they comprise 12 volunteer officers trained to use the kind of weaponry which is rarely seen on the streets of Britain, even in this age of terrorism. Among them are five former members of the Armed Forces – including one sergeant who was with the SAS – a former police diver, a former civilian staff call handler, and a former electrician. There are three members of the ethnic minorities, four officers under the age of 25, and one woman. Experiences within the unit are mixed: seven have yet to fire their weapons operationally, five have done so, and of those two have taken a life. In assessing suitability for this unit, a familiarity with weaponry is one of the least important requirements. That can be taught. The most important requirement is sound decision-making under pressure. That cannot be taught. Firearms officers are at the sharp end of modern policing, taking responsibility for split-second judgements of life and death, the implications and fallout of which will in almost all cases be pored over in the courts and newspapers for years afterwards.

As I watch them spill from their vehicles and jump out from the helicopter my fears for Catherine and our son only intensify. Body armour, helmets and military-grade weaponry are a part of the lexicon of death. And all I can do now is hope and watch.

Chief Superintendent Neil Fynn sits two streets away in the command van, universally referred to as The Enterprise. He is the gold commander for this incident, in overall charge. While he will prioritise beginning a dialogue with the hostage-takers, he will rely on Chief Inspector Pauline Callaghan, silver commander, and a team of 16 PCs to secure the streets outside the car park and keep the public away. Fynn has solid respect for Pauline, who at 52 has many years of experience of policing demonstrations and controlling public order. In the van with Fynn, two officers work a bank of screens. There are now two infrared micro-cameras along with two firearms officers on the roof of Mandela House, a block of council houses, opposite the car park. That gives a view into the cab of the Transit. There is a third camera and a directional microphone pointing out of the doorway of the car park stairwell, and a fourth suspended on a cable below the top floor of the car park. These two cameras show the rear doors of the van.

'Sir,' says Alison Courtney, a dark-haired communications specialist, veteran of many sieges. 'Fretwell has sent us a message on Twitter.' Sergeant Keith Gibson, sitting to her right looks over her shoulder at the screen and chuckles.

'What's it say then?' Fynn asks impatiently.

She reads it out.

> @GMPolice You've got 15 mins to get us a chopper or else. @MossSideM

'Ring him again, Sergeant,' Fynn sighs. 'Let's get to speak to him.' The phone rings out again for a full minute and is not answered.

'I'm definitely hearing the ringtone in the van,' Courtney says, with her hand to her headphones.

'How far away is Paddy Hamilton?' Fynn asks.

'Five minutes,' she replies.

Fynn looks at the monitors from the Mandela House cameras. Despite the lack of light from the car park, there is a clear heat signature from the van driver's seat, almost certainly Fretwell. He is an easy shot for the firearms officers. But it is the more confused warm background glow that seeps and flows behind him that complicates a shot. That is as likely to come from one of the hostages as from Cousins. Fynn speaks by radio to each of the six firearms officers in turn. His message is unequivocal: we shoot only when we have a clear headshot for both Fretwell *and* Cousins. Each officer acknowledges the rules of engagement. It becomes clear that only the two on Mandela House have a clear view of a target.

'Okay, send Fretwell a tweet. Asking to call us on this number.'

'Sir, I don't think that we should put this confidential number out into the Twittersphere,' Courtney says. 'It'll get jammed with hoax calls. Fretwell's message has already been retweeted 163 times. He's only got 267 followers but the Moss Side Mafia has 3,700. Any of them could start to interfere.'

'Good point, Alison. Social media is not my thing. Let's wait for Paddy.'

'The floodlights have arrived,' Gibson says

'Not before time. Let's get them mounted on the roof of the next block of flats, whatever that's called.'

'Thabo Mbeki House,' says Gibson.

'That will at least be too far for Fretwell or Cousins to shoot them out with a handgun… '

'Excuse me, sir, I've just found Fretwell's Facebook page,' Courtney interrupts. 'He has threatened to shoot both hostages in fifteen minutes unless we bring in a chopper to take them out of there. That was seven minutes ago.'

'Can I have a fag, Fretty?' Cousins asks.

'Fuck off.'

Cousins shrugs and slides a hand into his jeans pocket. He withdraws a small plastic ziplock bag with a number of green tablets in it. His eyes remain on Catherine as he taps out two into his palm, and then onto his tongue. His eyelids briefly flick shut as he swallows them. It reminds her of a wildlife documentary she had seen about lizards. Those pale brown eyes would suit any cold-blooded creature.

'We need food and something to drink, Fretty.'

Catherine nods her head, and risks eye contact with Cousins to mark her agreement. Her small smile is not returned. She wonders what those little green pills are doing to her captor.

'What we need is to get out of here,' Fretwell says, holding the phone to his head. 'The filth has left me a voicemail. They have finally seen what I posted on Facebook. Want us to phone them. Well, they can fuck off.'

Cousins sighs heavily. Catherine, trying to cement her connection to him says: 'If you ring them back they can arrange whatever you want. We can bring this to a resolution. And they will certainly bring you some cigarettes.' She offers Cousins a slight smile.

But he isn't looking at her face. He is staring at her breasts, and doesn't acknowledge her attempt to reach out to him.

Fretwell lights a cigarette and looks at his watch, before turning his face to his hostages. 'Well, it looks like you and your son have got about eight minutes left to live,' he says. It is the first time she has seen him grin, enough to see his yellow teeth. And it is perhaps the cruellest expression she has ever laid eyes on.

'They haven't lifted a finger to help you,' he says. 'No reply, nothing.' He looks back at the phone. 'Oh, I tell a lie. They just sent me a direct message on Facebook. "We can provide a helicopter but it will take time. We can send you some food and drink in the meantime. Please confirm the hostages are unharmed." They can piss off,' Fretwell says, turning off the phone and slipping it into his pocket.

Catherine feels compelled to speak: 'Why won't you talk to them? They have offered you what you want.'

Fretwell's face tightens as he stares at her. 'When I want your opinion I'll give it to you. In the meantime shut up, you stupid bitch. It's obviously a trap. The cops aren't going to give us a chopper, are they?'

'They might give us some food and a packet of fags,' Cousins says.

Fretwell turns to him with a face like thunder. 'You're no better than she is, arsehole. "Give me food give me drink give me fags".' His impersonation is camp and designed to be insulting. Cousins eyes him obliquely, the intimidation he suffers clear in his expression. It was only a short while ago that Fretwell's knife had been at his throat.

Catherine remains terrified. She is hungry, thirsty, and dying to go to the loo. But compared to her other predicament these are nothing. Fretwell seems set on killing her and Ethan despite the offers from the police. He has both gun and knife, and he seemed determined to engineer a disaster in which they will all be killed.

She has only one asset. She has very subtly begun to drive a wedge between the two criminals. But she will need more time to exploit it. And she isn't sure Cousins will ever have the courage to challenge Fretwell head-on.

Then something happens which makes everything a lot worse.

Ethan, already grizzling, now begins to wail loudly.

Patrick Hamilton's arrival brings a renewed sense of hope to the command van. Neil Fynn greets him warmly and briefs him on the latest developments.

'So he still isn't speaking to us?' Hamilton asks.

'No. He's playing silly buggers,' Gibson replies.

Hamilton has speed-read everything that is known about Liam Fretwell, and it does not incline him to optimism. So much about Fretwell's criminal record, gang activities, and interaction with the prison system speaks of a tendency towards psychopathy, unrestrained by rationality, planning or strategy. The upshot seems to be that Liam Fretwell is not a man whose actions can easily be predicted. Negotiation hinges on inducements, nudges, and concessions, but also relies on logic in the mind of the target. Someone as impulsive as Fretwell might easily choose a route of confrontation and violence even though he knows it to be worse. One prison officer had pithily summarised him as 'An awkward Arthur'.

'How many times have you rung him?' Hamilton asks.

'Five times,' Fynn says. 'The only response has been through social media.'

'Have you texted him?'

'No.'

'Right, let me try that. Fretwell may well lack confidence in verbal communication, at least that's what the psychiatrist's report seems to hint at. He's probably more at home in a more restricted format.'

'Righto,' Fynn responds.

Hamilton squeezes up on a chair at the screen next to Alison Courtney. He apologises for having to edge her to one side, and earns a warm smile in response. She shows him the smartphone numbers and email addresses they are using for the captors. He selects Fretwell's personal phone and then quickly types in a message, and hits send. 'Hopefully that will get us a response.'

> Liam, I've been asked to act as a go-between. Msg me and let's have a chat. Paddy

The message comes back quickly.

> Who the fck RU?

'Got a response,' Hamilton says.

Fynn leans in to have a look. 'Not exactly a positive one.'

'It's a start, that's all we need for now.' Hamilton begins to type again.

> Not a cop. Ex-army (Falklands), done time inside. Man U supporter. Giz a call?

'You've done time inside?' Fynn asks.

'Yep, four and a half months Bangui prison, Central African Republic. Not recommended. That's how I lost this,' he points at his glass eye. 'There was no trial, of course.'

'Good God,' Fynn responds, then rubs his chin ruminatively. He is a tall, ponderous man, with a pepper-and-salt beard and heavy-framed spectacles that add to his gravitas. 'So Fretwell supports Manchester United?'

'Fanatically, according to our records. I'm pretty agnostic

myself, but I can remember a few key players from my time, in case we have to start a discussion. And I would like to have a discussion.'

'What about Cousins?'

Hamilton nods. 'A different kettle of fish altogether. Junior to Fretwell in the Moss Side Mafia, so I expect Fretwell to be calling the shots. But Cousins is ambitious and just as evil, having seen his record of sexual offences. He's sly, twisted and creepy. I must say I rather fear for Catherine Blake.'

I was looking at Catherine in her sleep just two days ago. She was curled on her right side away from me, her breathing deep and even. I was lying curled around her, and in my usual position with one hand in front of my face, resting gently on the springy bundle of her hair to stop it tickling my face and neck. She is a much lighter sleeper than I am, awake in a millisecond when Ethan needs her. So it is a precious moment to see Catherine asleep. The crease of concern across her eyelids is gone, the little moue of tension that slightly twists her mouth cannot be seen. The milky freckled skin of that delightful shoulder flexes gently with her breath. There is now an unfathomable sadness about this recollection, and the embracing warmth that I am now denied. There is so much that I wanted to do, so much I want to say to her, that are now just inaudible ghostly whispers breezing into her ear, perhaps the seeds of dreams, Sandman's grains for her eyes.

For as I say this, I know what is to come next.

Chapter Eight

I had my own run-in with the gangs of Manchester when I was newly qualified probation officer. It wasn't a particularly rough area, or so I had thought. I was on my way to visit a woman who had just been given a caution for her third offence of shoplifting. We suspected that it wasn't primarily the inability to budget that had caused the single mum to run out of food for her two children, but an expensive drug habit for which she was resisting getting help.

She and her brood lived off one of those long fenced-in urban alleyways in Oldham which are choked with wheelie bins and dumped rubbish. There were barriers at either end to prevent cyclists making it a cut through, but as it trimmed a good hundred yards off the road route it was inevitably well used by those on two wheels.

It was 10.45 a.m. and I was early for the appointment. I heard the whirr of wheels only in the last three seconds before a cyclist whizzed past, knocking my briefcase. It was a black lad of about 12 or 13 on one of those saddle-less BMX bikes. He was wearing a puffa jacket and a woollen hat. I was well aware that we were no longer in the era where a man in the street can berate a youngster simply because of the authority of age. The deference to adults that I experienced as a child is long gone, and may never have applied in some places. But I was cross, and used only the precaution of distance. So it was only when the lad was 30 yards past me that I shouted: 'Look where you're going. You shouldn't even be cycling here.'

What I had expected, I suppose, was a volley of swearing, or perhaps a raised single finger for my trouble. Honour would have been vaguely satisfied on both sides. Somehow I got it very wrong.

The cyclist squealed to a halt, turned to look at me and asked: 'You dissing me?'

I said nothing. Standing on the pedals, he began to cycle slowly back towards me. My height, my suit, my clearly official business – none of that fazed him at all. I was torn between the ridiculous cowardice of running away or making some pathetic verbal excuse to soften my challenge to him. Instead the vestiges of my anger and a streak of stubbornness made me stay. Two yards away the boy stepped off the bike and let it fall to the pavement. He was perhaps 5-foot-4, athletic looking and had a lolly stick protruding from his mouth. Was he really going to fight me? Did he have a knife? Was I going to be stabbed for such a trivial piece of assertiveness? He stood with his hands in his pockets and stared up at me, the white stick being moved left to right and back again in his mouth.

At that moment I heard another bike behind me, and turned

to see a second lad, bigger and maybe a year older than the first. Lad one said to me: 'Give me your phone.' He said it in such a confident and natural way, as if it would be unthinkable to refuse. He even clicked his fingers when I hesitated.

'And your wallet.' This from the second boy.

Neither had shown me a weapon, but it was their self-confidence that disarmed me. I pulled out the phone, it was nothing fancy. But I didn't want to lose my wallet and procrastinated just a moment too long. The punch in the face from lad number two took me by surprise, and the shock rather than the pain made me reel against a high wooden fence behind me. Boy number one kicked me, probably aiming for my groin but connecting, agonisingly, with my kneecap. I sat down hard, and did nothing to stop them taking both wallet and phone. They made a cursory attempt to open the briefcase. It was one of those lightweight plastic jobs, finished to look like metal. It was way stronger than I had expected. After cracking his heel down on the lock, and seeing it fail to open, lad number two picked it up and threw it high over a broken-glass topped brick wall into some industrial yard. They then cycled away, so casually relaxed that they freewheeled most of the way, with barely a backwards glance.

I hobbled my way back to a newsagents near where I had parked the car, and got them to ring the police. It was only then, when asked what had happened, that I realised that the easiest way to encapsulate my experience was one simple word: mugging. Fortunately I had my car keys, still in my jacket pocket, and was about to return to the vehicle when the lady at the newsagents said, 'I think you've sat in some dog dirt.'

There was one saving grace to the day, and that was being able to retrieve my briefcase from the car repair yard where it had been thrown. In return for describing my story to the proprietor I had to listen to his own racially charged interpretation of Britain's descent into criminality. He was trying to be sympathetic of course, and I let it pass. If there is a moral to this story I suppose it is pick your fights carefully.

But then some fights just pick you, as Catherine discovered.

Paddy Hamilton watches Fretwell's developing narrative on Facebook over Alison Courtney's shoulder. The photograph of Catherine and her child, clearly terrified, cowed in some claustrophobic corner of a Ford Transit. The comment above: 'Cheeky cow what dissed us. Suggestions bro's?'

'He's canvassing the gang for punishments,' Courtney says.

'There's thirty-two likes already,' Hamilton says.

Courtney puts a hand hurriedly over her mouth. 'Oh God. Someone suggested cutting her throat. And another said "rape her ass".'

'Close it down,' Fynn orders. 'Get Facebook to take that account offline immediately. If the press discover this it will be a PR disaster.'

'I'm on it,' responds Gibson. 'I spoke to them earlier. It might still take ten minutes.'

'This has been a grave error of judgement, frankly,' Fynn says. 'I was persuaded that social media may have been a route to open negotiations, but Fretwell has just used it to threaten and gloat.'

Hamilton assumes that Fynn has seen Fretwell's earlier Facebook comment in which a photograph of the Chief Constable of Greater Manchester had been copied from their own website underneath the comment: 'I am the nonce and wanker-in-chief.'

'I do apologise for my part in this,' Hamilton says. Alison Courtney had initially suggested letting Fretwell have free reign on the Internet, but he doesn't want her to take the blame alone. 'It has sometimes worked in the past, but clearly there are disadvantages.'

Hamilton overhears an officer on Fynn's radio say that the lights are ready to go on. 'Neil, can I suggest you hold off on the lights for a few minutes. It could panic them—'

'Something's happening inside the van,' Courtney interrupts, holding headphones close to her ears. She turns on the mic, and the command truck is filled with distressing sound of violence, threats, and repeated booming noises.

'Oh God. He's killing them both,' she says.

Fynn speaks into his radio: 'Kilo Lima one and two, report target status. Over. '

'Negative, gold leader. He's in the back. We need the lights on. All we've got is generalised heat background, over.'

'I can hear crying,' Courtney says. 'Female and baby, quite clear.'

'Well at least they're alive. We've got to stabilise this, and damn quickly,' Fynn says, shaking his head. 'I'm pretty much ready to storm the vehicle.'

'I'd like to try another attempt at calling Fretwell. This time I'll try the hostage's phone.' He gets up to go into the soundproof booth to make the call. Fynn and Courtney will be listening in on headphones.

This is what just happened. Ethan Blake cannot be quieted. Catherine is shushing and jiggling him, but the combination of being hungry for the solid food he would normally get at this time of day, and not being allowed to roam free is just too much. He refuses her breast, and after wriggling and kicking, she puts him down on the grimy carpet between her legs. Now he just sits there and wails, the sound whining like a buzz saw around the inside of the van.

'I've told you before, keep him shut up!' Fretwell yells, not looking up from his phone.

'He's tired, and he's hungry,' Catherine says. 'I'm doing the best I can.'

Fretwell glances at his watch 'Suppose we've only got to put up with it for five minutes anyway, eh Jazz?'

'Yeah. Then we can shoot 'em both.'

'I reckon we should execute the kid first,' Fretwell says casually, still working away on his phone. 'So that they can see we really mean business.'

'Yeah, that's right,' Cousins says.

Catherine fights an engulfing terror, and the almost overwhelming desire to beg for her child's life. She is cornered and angry. A deep breath, then through gritted teeth she says what she has been getting prepared to say for almost an hour: 'I promise you that if you shoot at my child I will go for you with nails, teeth, everything I have. You can murder me, like you murdered my husband, I don't care anymore. But if you hurt Ethan you are going to have to deal with me. Do you understand?'

Cousins stares open-mouthed at her, then his eyes slide towards Fretwell from whom he is clearly expecting some kind of response. Fretwell takes his time, doesn't look up but remains sitting in the driver's seat, working away on the phone. A minute passes and there is still nothing said. But the atmosphere is crackling with tension.

When action comes it is swift and terrifying.

Fretwell vaults over the seats, grabs Catherine under the chin and heaves her to her feet as if she weighs nothing. With both hands he then slams her head half a dozen times against a sharp stanchion which buttress the frame of the van, then throws her to the floor.

It is finished in ten seconds, but the blood from her gashed face and torn ear smear the inside of the panels. Fretwell bellows every vile word that has ever been used by a man to degrade a woman and then adds: 'Don't you never, never dis me again. I'll kill you in a heartbeat.'

My Catherine, my brave, beautiful wife, lies stunned on the floor. Ethan, who had tumbled from her arms in the first seconds of the assault, sucks in a huge breath. He hasn't yet cried but looks up astonished, bright blue eyes scanning the face of the human being who has just upended the benign universe he thought he inhabited. This attack on his mother is just too big for tears. While she sobs silently, curled up at the back of the van, he levers himself laboriously to his tiny feet, Lugs in his hand and calls: 'Mamma?'

Catherine cannot voice discernible words through the blood and saliva but lifts her head and begins to crawl the three feet to her son. As she does so, Ethan holds out the stuffed rabbit to her for comfort, and takes two faltering independent hands-free steps towards his mother.

They are his first ever.

She enfolds him in her arms and there begins a rising ululation of their conjoined tears, almost perfectly synchronised, his an octave or two above hers. Catherine hides Ethan within the folds of her arms and glares up at her assailant. The hair on the right-hand side of her head is matted with blood and mucus, and there are trails, partially wiped, down her chin, her nose and the side of her head. One eye is almost shut and a bruise is beginning which will be the size of a goose egg.

This is not any longer a woman that I recognise. Drawn out from within there is an expression of determination on her face that was never needed within the years of our marriage, nor even during her worst years in the school playground. It is almost an extrusion of ancestral resources, woven into her DNA millennia ago. Her eyes are feral, her teeth bared, her tongue pinkly visible. For the first time I realise that she is plumbing the same levels of desperation as her captors, living moment by moment, minute by minute. The same way they do.

'I meant every word,' she wheezes.

It is just quiet enough that Fretwell can pretend that he hasn't heard it.

But he has. And he lets it go.
And then Catherine's phone rings.
He answers it.

Chapter Nine

Fretwell holds the phone to his ear, and slides down in the back of the Transit. 'Yeah?'

'Paddy Hamilton here, Liam. It's time for a chat.'

'Right. Move those fuckers off the roof opposite…'

'Liam, there are all sorts of things we can do for you and your friend in there. We just need to establish a few principles to make sure there is no confusion, right? My role is a bit like a centre half. I'm getting plenty of instruction from the dugout behind me, if you follow. But what happens on the pitch is about you and me understanding each other.'

'We've got a bitch and her kid in here, and we gave you a deadline. And we ain't heard nothing. Get those fuckers off the roof. '

'About the deadline,' Hamilton sighs. 'It took a long time to realise you were posting on Facebook. We tried to ring, as you know. So okay, I'm told we can get you out of there by chopper. But it will take a while to organise. So give us a break, okay? No more deadlines.'

'Fuck off. If I feel like giving them a bullet, I fucking well will.'

'I hear you, Liam. Right now I need to know they are okay.'

'You're fine, aintcha?' Fretwell has clearly turned towards the captives, but Hamilton can't hear any response from them.

'I need to speak to Catherine Blake, Liam. It's important for us to know how she is.'

'Fuck off.' Fretwell then addresses the hostages directly. 'I'm treating you all right, ain't I?'

Hamilton hears a murmur that might be assent.

'Louder, bitch.' There was a sound of a blow, a gasp, and a bout of tears from the child.

'I'm fine, we're being treated well.' The woman's voice is surprisingly composed, Hamilton thinks, though there is a trembling sub-tone to it.

'So like I said, get those wankers off the roof,' Fretwell says, raising his voice over Ethan's wailing.

'Liam. There are some things I can do for you back here, and there are some I just can't, mate. I'll keep working on the obstinate buggers back here for you, and I'll let you know. In the meantime I've ordered some pizza and burgers for you, and some coke. All right?'

There is some conversation which he can't catch then another male voice which he takes to be Cousins shouts: 'Two packs of Mayfair king-size, and some cans of Red Bull.' On the screen in front of him Hamilton spies an instant message from Fynn:

Clear bead Cousins. Fretwell sporadically. Just say the word.

Hamilton only has to say a single word to trigger the firearms squad. That word is 'Barcelona'. It is intended to be used only when negotiations reach an impasse. It is a mark of pride for Paddy Hamilton that in his entire career he had never needed to do that.

'All right Liam, and Janile if you can hear me, the food will be coming up in five minutes. But I also need to know what Catherine needs for the baby,' Hamilton says.

'Piss off. They'll get what they're given. I want Pizza Hut not Domino's. Hawaiian with extra pineapple. Make sure there's plenty of ketchup on the burgers, and proper fries.'

Hamilton picks up Gibson's acknowledgement through the headphones. 'Okay, Liam, I've passed that lot on. Might delay the pizza a bit. I'd still really like to talk to Catherine if I may.'

'Fuck off. When you deliver the food, I don't want some armed fucking copper bringing it over, right? Get it brought to the top of the stairs and pushed out where we can see it. I'll send the woman out to pick it up.'

'That sounds like a plan. I'll call you again in ten minutes when I know about the helicopter. By the way, where do you want to be taken?' Hamilton tries to make it sound as casual as possible.

'None of your fucking business, innit?'

'Well, that's true, but if you take a helicopter you have to file a flight plan with air traffic control and all that kind of stuff. If the first the pilot knows about the destination is when you get in, it will delay you. And we wouldn't want those kind of details getting in the way of a smooth departure.'

'You don't give a shit about whether or not we get away.'

'I certainly care about the safety of the hostages, so if allowing you a clean getaway is the price of saving two innocent lives, then I am happy to do it.'

Hamilton can't hear what Fretwell seems to be saying. But he is delighted that contact has been made and, for all of Fretwell's angry and foul-mouthed tirades, he is listening. The phone goes dead. He turns round and sees Fynn standing behind him grinning. 'You've done very well Paddy, I'm really impressed.'

'Early days, Neil. Fretwell is clearly in charge and he's just as nasty a bastard as we expected. God knows what it was that he did to Catherine Blake.'

Fynn blows a sigh of agreement. 'She is the most important unknown quantity. If she is picking up the food, presumably with the baby as a hostage, there may be a chance to give her some information. I'm having that prepared now.'

'On one job in the Cameroon we were able to get a gun in with food,' Hamilton says. 'The hostages were local policemen. That wouldn't work here, but you might consider pepper spray or CS gas.'

Fynn shakes his head. 'Absolutely not. We can't do that. Anything Fretwell found on her would jeopardise her survival, and that of the baby. It's not our job to put such a huge responsibility in the hands of someone who is untrained, already terrified, and just trying to save her child.'

'Okay, your call,' Hamilton says.

'Paddy, it's my job to see all the worst outcomes. But as you know, the most reliable one is to just wear them down, tire them out, and sap their will. In the meantime if we get two clear shots, I'm going to authorise it.'

The gold commander is not completely out of resources. The secret weapon he has demanded is arriving. When an unmarked Vauxhall estate pulls up at the perimeter of the police cordon, silver commander Pauline Callaghan has some difficulty believing that the driver, a long-haired young man in a Black Sabbath T-shirt, studded with facial piercings, is as he claims responding to an urgent call from her boss. But when she radios Fynn he responds with: 'Thank God, finally. Let him through.' She stands aside and watches as the car slides in beside the command van. The skinny driver emerges and begins to ease out two metallic trunks from the back, the kind that might belong to a photographer. To most uniformed coppers, Gareth Hoddle looks just the sort of choice individual who might be found on a violent demonstration or doing small-scale cannabis dealing. So Callaghan is even more surprised when she sees Fynn go out and warmly greet him. She can't imagine what he has to offer. She reckons she is a good judge of character, and to her Hoddle looks like he belongs behind bars.

Callaghan's judgement isn't far off. Four years ago Gareth Hoddle was imprisoned for six months after being caught with a home-made drone which he was using to fly drugs into Long Lartin high security jail in Worcestershire where his brother Michael was serving three years for assault. Ministry of Justice experts who examined the tiny and almost silent drone were impressed with the innovations Hoddle had made to improve the original commercial model. He was clearly an electronics genius. In what must be regarded as a very successful piece of rehabilitation, Hoddle was offered early release and persuaded by his probation officer to act as a consultant for the Home Office developing a drone- killing drone. In six months of testing at Wandsworth Prison, Hoddle's Whisperkill device intercepted 17 drugs and mobile phone consignments which would otherwise have made it to the cell windows of the Victorian-era building. Hoddle's used a microphone attuned to the noise of drones to find them, even in darkness, and then drape an entangling net into their rotors.

But it was a second device, developed as a hobby, that attracted the interest of the police. Betty, as Hoddle called her, was a cheap radio-controlled toy car less than six inches long. Stripped of its chassis, with silent rubber wheels and a noise-suppressed motor, Betty had two directional rotors made from the necks of plastic bottles which enabled it to fly nimbly, or when turned horizontally to simply power it along any smooth surface. With the electric motor set for crawl speed, and with a powerful microphone and micro-camera, Betty could safely sneak up close to hostage takers without being noticed.

Today was the first time she had been used in a siege.

It is after six p.m. and the fuzzy, maroon twilight that passes for night in the city has seeped into every corner. Police marksmen lie motionless on the roof of Mandela house, still looking for a risk-free opportunity to terminate the siege. But for more than five minutes now they have had nothing but a vague heat glow in their night scopes to guide them. Fretwell and Cousins are sitting on the floor in the back of the van, opposite Catherine. Ethan is asleep, in his mother's lap. Having seen the police marksmen on the roof, the captors are unwilling to spend much time in the front seats. Fretwell hung up on the negotiator a couple of minutes before, and is busily checking his phone.

'I hope they hurry up with that grub,' Cousins says. 'I'm starving.' His sallow face has acquired a laziness since he took the tablets. Catherine has been willing him to fall asleep, but wonders what she would do if he does. There are few obvious options. Fretwell has retained the gun, which is now carefully stowed in the pocket of his hoodie.

'Oi. My Facebook account has been blocked,' Fretwell says. 'Bastards.'

Since the phone call the tension in the van has eased. Catherine has been biding her time for 20 minutes, but finally she has to speak. 'I'm afraid I really have to go to the loo. I'm absolutely bursting.'

Fretwell stares at her as if she is a lower form of life. He sighs, turns to Cousins and says: 'Should have put nappies on 'em both.'

Cousins sniggers. 'Right, man.'

'There might be a toilet off the stairwell,' she says. 'I won't be long.'

'Forget it,' Fretwell says, absentmindedly. He peers over the backs of the seats and out of the windscreen. He can make out activity on the roof of another building to his left, which could only be cops. A decision congeals in his mind. He slithers rapidly over the seat back and behind the wheel, starts the engine and bangs the van into reverse. He backs sharply into the interior of the car park, out of sight of the roof. He shifts into first, then accelerates down a ramp to a split-floor half a storey lower, but on the other side of the car park. He eases the vehicle next to an interior wall within sight of the glass door of the pedestrian exit, and hits the brake. In the headlamps he glimpses two black-clad figures jumping for cover into the stairwell.

'That's put the wind up them,' Fretwell says. 'They can't see us from outside now.'

'Good thinking, Fretty,' says Cousins.

Fretwell throws open the driver's side door, sprints to the back of the van, and pulls open the door. 'You, out,' he points at Catherine. 'Leave the kid there, go to the edge where I can see you. You've got 60 seconds. Don't try anything funny.' With index finger and thumb he mimes shooting Ethan.

Catherine sets Ethan down gently, trying not to wake him, and scrambles out of the door. Fretwell tugs her out as if she is a sack of potatoes and she stumbles, her knee hitting the cold, hard concrete floor. After so long in one position in the van she can barely stand but hobbles in the direction she was told.

She barely has time to release her trousers and pants before her bladder gives out, and she groans with the relief. As she comes up from the squat, she glances over the concrete parapet and down into the streets, three floors below. The roads are jammed with police vehicles, and blue lights flash reflections in the windows of the flats around them. Further back are crowds of onlookers. On this side there are no flats high enough to give a view into the car park. Fretwell has been very clever. She pulls her clothing back up, and takes a quick look at her watch. Is that a minute yet? She isn't sure.

Then from the van comes a single, sickening gunshot.

Chapter Ten

Never before has a hostage raced back into captivity. 'No! No! Ethan!' Her screams throw ripples of harsh laughter around the concrete as she sprints back to the van. The door is partially open, and Fretwell hauls her in. Ethan's shrieks of terror deny her worst fears. She dives for him and squeezes him in her arms. 'It's okay my darling, Mummy is back, Mummy would never leave you, I promise.'

Cousins laughs and shakes his head. Fretwell holds the gun, from the barrel of which a gaseous blue ribbon drifts upwards. There is a ragged hole in the side panel of the van a good three feet above Ethan's head. Catherine stares at the hole, back at the gun and up into Fretwell's grinning countenance. 'What are you doing?' she gasps.

'Bitches always take too long in the toilet. I thought I'd hurry you up.'

Catherine's mouth hangs open and her breath comes raggedly. That they could so cruelly do this to her is even now a horrible revelation.

For some reason it never occurred to CS Neil Fynn that Fretwell and Cousins would just move the van within the car park. He could kick himself for failing to anticipate how much more difficult that has made his job. Neither of the sharpshooters on the roof of Mandela House can now see anything of the vehicle. There are no equivalent buildings on the other side of the car park to use instead. The nearest is a three-storey Victorian warehouse, converted on first and second floors into flats and on the top floor to an architect's studio. This is largely open plan space, and retains the pitched roof and extensive skylights, but is a little below level III where the van is. Fynn sends an officer to scout out the possibilities but is quickly told there is no line of sight to where the Transit is parked. The four firearms officers who had earlier been dropped by helicopter onto the car park's open top floor are able to move down one further storey which puts them in sight of the rear of the van 40 yards away. Though the car park's strip lighting is still on near the van, there are too few parked vehicles for them to approach for a safe view.

They are half an hour into the siege. 'We've really got to nail those bastards,' Gibson says. 'I can't imagine the worry that Mrs Blake is feeling for her baby.'

Alison Courtney concurs. She has heard through the directional mic every shout, every baby's sob, and every bang from the van. She is set for at least a 12 hour shift, but already her nerves are frayed. 'I've got PC Amy Parrish to accumulate everything that a new mum might need. I just hope that we can get these items through with the food.'

Paddy Hamilton is just finishing a coronation chicken sandwich that someone had left for him on his desk. This was in his experience just the early stages of the siege, in which the captors and the forces of law and order established communication and enough of a rapport to move things to the next level. Despite Fretwell's piece of inspiration in moving the van, the fatigue, the tension and the tiredness would all begin to exact their toll. For all Gibson's impatience, everything that Hamilton had learned in the 17 sieges where he had been a negotiator over the last dozen years told him that avoiding bringing matters to a head was the surest route to a successful outcome.

Hamilton wipes his mouth with a napkin, and retrieves a piece of chicken from between his teeth. 'Neil, next time I speak to them they are bound to ask about the chopper. What are your thoughts?'

'The Chief Constable is naturally reluctant. We do have one available, but if they insist on taking the hostages with them then we would no longer be able to control what happens in flight. It just makes the stakes a lot higher.'

'Understood. So we need some believable excuses when it doesn't show up.'

'There is still delay, obviously,' Fynn says. 'We need to know the destination, and could be various technical considerations we could use.'

'But in the end they will suss out that we're stringing them along. So it would be useful to at least have available the police helicopter to buzz the building again. They won't know that it's the wrong chopper, and we will at least be appearing to fulfil our side of the bargain. The rapport, such as it is, that I have built with Fretwell won't survive a realisation that I have been lying. I might be playing the role of a go-between, but there's only so much that I can blame on you.'

'Fair enough,' Fynn says.

'Okay, I'm going to ring him now.' Hamilton makes his way to the communication booth, and punches up Fretwell's number.

Fretwell's mobile rings. This time he answers it quickly. 'Cop wankers' helpline, how can I assist?'

'Highly original,' Hamilton says, then, adding an edge of steel to his voice, 'let off another shot like that and I won't be able to stop them coming for you.'

'You can fuck off.'

'If the hostages appear to be in imminent danger, there will be nothing that I can do for you. Do you understand?'

'I don't give a toss, mate. I've not believed a word you've said right from the start. There's no helicopter, not even any nosh.'

'The food's on its way, I told you. Literally two minutes. Now I have to tell you something. The helicopter will be half an hour, and we still need your destination, okay?'

'We need to go to Rio. We'll take the chopper to Manchester Airport. You lay on a flight from there to Rio tonight.'

Hamilton sighs. 'Liam, things have changed a bit in Brazil since Ronnie Biggs' day. We have an extradition treaty with them now, you know?'

'Do I care?'

Hamilton takes a moment to think. In the midst of Fretwell's brooding silence at the other end he can make out a baby's gurgling noise. The boy sounds happy, or at least content. He suddenly feels a wave of optimism that the siege can be safely ended after all. Better still, he just been screen-topped by Gibson to say the food is finally on its way up.

'Liam? The food is waiting for you at the top of the stairs.'

'Right. I don't want to see a single member of the filth anywhere on this floor, right? No one is to talk to the bitch when I send her out. No messages, no little tricks. And one more thing. If you have put anything in the nosh, remember we will be feeding it to the kid first. A fucking Mickey Finn would kill him, and it would be your fault, right?'

'We would never do anything like that, Liam.'

'Fucking sure you wouldn't.' Fretwell coughs his scepticism and ends the call.

Fretwell turns and stares over the seat towards Catherine. 'Right. You know what to do. Go to the top of the stairs. Pick up the food and come straight back, right? I can watch you through here.' He taps the windscreen. 'Do not go out of the beam of the headlights. If you see a cop anywhere, right, you come straight back here and tell me. Forget the fucking food, just come back here straightaway. Right?'

Catherine nods. This will be the fourth time that she has left our precious Ethan with these two, and the weight of guilt about doing it is not getting any lighter. She just has to get through each new hurdle, doing the right thing, not taking any chances, and things will improve. She has to believe that. Cousins, she notices, seems almost in a daze. She presumes that the two tablets have done that. If that means she has only one effective captor, then so much the better.

Fretwell seemed to be thinking along similar lines. He cuffs Cousins across the head and shouts at him. 'Wake up, you idle motherfucker.'

'What's the matter?' Cousins asks.

'You've done fuck all, that's what's the matter. Sit in the front, keep an eye on both those wing mirrors while I let her out.'

Cousins gets up and slides over into the passenger seat. Fretwell cracks the driver's door an inch or two, takes a quick look around then jogs to the back and opens the door. Catherine is waiting and ready.

She spots the food the moment she walks around the front of the van. Two pizza boxes, and on top of them a large grease-stained paper bag. As she opens the reinforced glass door and steps into the landing she looks down and sees a sheet of paper pinned under the pizza boxes. In marker pen capitals it says:

KEEP ABSOLUTELY STILL, CATHERINE. **DO NOT RAISE YOUR HEAD.** NOW LIFT YOUR EYES RIGHT AND YOU WILL SEE US. SAY NOTHING WHEN YOU GET BACK. IF SHOTS ARE FIRED LIE FLAT IN THE VAN WITH ETHAN IN YOUR ARMS. WE WILL AIM HIGH. YOU WILL FIND MILK, YOGHURT AND A BANANA IN THE BAG. GOOD LUCK. DISCARD THIS MESSAGE.

As her eyes adjust to the gloom she makes out two body-armoured and helmeted officers crouching in the shadows half a floor up, their assault rifles pointing over her head. Between them crouches a woman officer, under-armoured by comparison, with a headset and mic over her blonde ponytailed hair. She stares directly into Catherine's eyes and has a single finger in front of her lips, her eyes wide in emphasis.

Catherine tosses the message aside and peers into the bag. There are three burgers, cigarettes, a carton of half-fat milk, a pack of Red Bull, baby-size yoghurts, wet wipes and a toilet roll twinpack. She picks everything up and starts to walk back. Through the glass security door she can make out Fretwell aiming the pistol at her, from the gap created by the partially opened driver's door.

'Give it to me,' he says, guiding her to the back of the van and pushing her inside. He climbs in afterwards, the door still partially open.

Catherine is shocked by what she sees. Ethan is standing between Cousins' outstretched legs, holding on to his raised knee for support. He shows her Lugs by way of greeting and says, 'Mamma come.' He looks very pleased with himself and sits down. He has clearly been crawling around in her absence and is now filthy. There are dirty smears across his face, down his nappy and along his legs. She scoops him up into her arms, and kisses him on the forehead.

'Who's a messy little boy then?'

Fretwell rifles through the package. He slides a pizza box to Cousins, and then tosses him a can of Red Bull. For himself he takes a huge bite of a burger. Melted cheese and ketchup slide down his chin. Ethan stares over Catherine's shoulder at the burger and stretches his arm towards his captor.

'Greedy little fucker, ain't he?' Fretwell notes.

'He's not had anything solid to eat all day.' She had eaten nothing herself since she shared a yoghurt and banana with her son in the morning. The gun is now stowed in Fretwell's waistband while he eats. There is no sign of the knife. Another opportunity, she knows it. But what chance has she of being able to barge out through the still-open van door with Ethan in her arms? She wonders what the police are doing, and how ultimately they plan to rescue them. It probably will all come down to more time, everyone getting worn down. That would not be good for Ethan. He has the least patience, the least understanding. It would be awful.

Fretwell takes the package of food, backs out of the van, slams the rear door shut and jumps into the driver's seat.

'Can I have a yoghurt for my son?'

Fretwell stares at her. 'I chucked all that shit out.' He fishes in the bag, and passes across a greasy burger, its paper wrapping already translucent, over the seat back towards the child. 'You want a fucking burger, Ethan, dontcha? If you wanted milk and stuff you would have grabbed your mum's tit, right?'

Ethan glances up at his mother as if somehow he knows he isn't supposed to have a burger, but he reaches out for it anyway. Catherine tries to intercept it but Fretwell pulls it back. 'Nah, I'm giving it to him, not to you.'

'The mother taking food from her kid's mouth,' Cousins says, his first contribution for some time.

'That greasy meat isn't good for him,' Catherine says. 'We don't feed him anything that rich. He's too young.'

'Bollocks. He wants what he wants. It never did me any harm.' Fretwell pulls out the pistol and presses the tip of the barrel to Catherine's head. 'Move to the back of the van, bitch. And leave the kid where he is.'

Catherine complies. Ethan looks at her, his face creased in the distress he picks up from her, and he begins to cry. Fretwell climbs over the seat into the back, and crouches down to offer him the burger. It is way too big for his tiny hands, so Fretwell unwraps the paper in front of the child. 'There, look at that, eh? Fucking magic.'

Ethan stops crying. He reaches for the burger and pulls the top half of the bun towards him, dragging onions, ketchup, mustard and dill pickle up his leg. He takes a small bite of the bread, and three chews later is pushing it out of his mouth with his tongue. Fretwell breaks off a bit of the meat patty and with his fingers offers it to the child. Ethan puts it in his mouth, and then turns to look questioningly at his mother. She smiles back at him. Ethan looks at Cousins and Fretwell in turn, and then turns to where Lugs is lying next to him. He grabs the now grease-stained rabbit by the head, pushes the piece of burger meat out with his tongue and into his hand. He then gurgles something, and offers the meat to the stuffed animal. 'Ugs dins,' he says, triumphantly.

Catherine can see Cousins grinning away. 'Fucking bunny getting well fed!' Even Fretwell seems amused by this. He's no longer pointing the gun at her, and gradually slips it back into his waistband.

'You do have the water still, don't you?' she asks.

'Nah. Drank it.' He still seems to get great delight from small acts of spite. 'You can have this.' He digs up a can of Red Bull and tosses it towards her. She fumbles her catch and the tin clangs against the metal panel of the rear door.

'I'm anxious enough without loading up on caffeine,' she says.

'Your choice.' Fretwell looks smug.

Catherine takes the tin, clicks open the ring pull and takes a hesitant swig. In her prejudice she has never tasted an energy drink before, and it is even more saccharine than she expects. She suppresses a grimace, and takes a second longer pull. She needs fluids.

Ethan has distributed pieces of burger and onion all over his face and hands and onto Lugs. It isn't clear how much of it he has actually eaten, but the sheer process of having food in his mouth seems to quieten him.

Fretwell and Cousins are having a belching competition, each attempting to surpass the other in the noise and duration of each eructation. Catherine can taste their pungent breath, and it is making her bilious. Cousins has eaten an entire pizza, bar two slices which Fretwell snatches away with a triumphant giggle. Even here, with enough food to go round, Fretwell is determined to establish his dominance. Ethan seems to be fascinated by the two men and stares open-mouthed at them. After one particularly lengthy burp by Fretwell, Ethan giggles and bangs his hand in the remains of the ketchup.

While Ethan works his puckish and mucky charm on the captors, Catherine gradually eases herself back from the rear of the van, and finally sits with her arms protectively on the shoulders of her son. She does what she so often does at home and eats the various far-flung pieces of Ethan's burger, at least those which have avoided ending up on the carpet or oil-stained van floor. Her grazed face still stings, and she can feel an enormous bruise building along her cheekbone. For all that, the last ten minutes of eating have been the least stressful since the abduction began. She is a little surprised that the police haven't taken advantage of the distraction of food to launch an assault. She keeps in mind how she would grab Ethan and dive to the floor at the first sign of shooting.

Back in the stairwell PC Philippa Caldicot is crouching down behind the partial cover of the banister on the half landing above level III. To either side of her are the reassuring armoured presences of PCs Michael O'Donnell and Iain Searle, Heckler and Koch assault rifles at the ready. The cold fluorescent light above them has been due to be turned off for more than an hour, but the electrician doing the job on the ground floor hasn't been able to isolate the correct circuit because the labels were only written in marker pen and some time in the intervening years the ink has rubbed off. So for now the three officers have to put up with buzz, a flicker and the occasional flash of darkness. Fortunately the reach of the Transit's headlamps only goes as far as the fifth step up towards them. McDonald, something of an amateur car mechanic, has a theory.

'They're not running the engine,' he whispers. 'That van's late

1990s. Probably only got the one battery. Good chance it will be flat as a pancake in a few hours.'

'They won't like that,' hisses Searle, with a grin.

'What's bad for them isn't necessarily good for the hostages,' mutters Caldicot. 'How are you going to see who to shoot if we have to storm the van?' she adds.

Gareth Hoddle is sitting cross-legged on the floor of the car park immediately underneath where the Transit is parked on the floor above. In front of him is an open attaché case in which his remote control console is set, its long aerial fully extended. He carefully sets Betty down, pointing her ahead of him towards the ramp which leads up a half floor. The workings and wheels are carefully camouflaged with torn strips of grubby polythene and bin bag, and only the thin matte-grey painted aerial shows that it is not a piece of windblown litter. A firearms officer kneels on each side, weapons cocked and ready. Hoddle has carefully checked every circuit on Betty, and made a few test drives on the car park surface. There is no significant noise even when it traverses the raised yellow paint rumble strips. He checks in on his police radio with the gold commander, and getting the okay initialises the vehicle on the console. The device creeps silently across the floor, and up the ramp. Looking into the console Hoddle can see an infrared image of this higher floor of the car park. He pushes left and right control levers forward, and though he can no longer see it, the camera shows Betty is heading steadily towards the next up-ramp 30 metres away. On his headphones he is hoping to catch anything that is picked up by her powerful microphone, but apart from the background noise from the street, and the distant rumble of traffic, there is nothing. He pauses Betty, radios in to Fynn and awaits final approval.

Chief Superintendent Fynn has not been idle. He has placed an officer with powerful binoculars on the ninth floor of an office block half a mile away, but for all that distance it still gives the best view into the interior of the car park. An officer with a state-of-the-art sniper's rifle is next to him. There are five members of a firearms unit now in the stairwell where the food had been, and four spaced around the higher floor. There is no shortage of firepower. The problem is the same as from the start. The two hostage-takers are rarely in the crosshairs together, and never for more than a few seconds. Fynn has a supply of stun grenades, smoke grenades, blindingly bright lights, and an Israeli-made machine that has yet to be used by his force which would focus an insufferable volume of noise into a small area. In each case it is quite unclear how such weaponry could be used without putting the hostages at risk.

It is seven o'clock, close to the moment when the promised helicopter is supposed to arrive to whisk Fretwell and Cousins off to a life of supposed freedom and luxury in Brazil. Hamilton looks at his watch and marshals the available excuses for its non-arrival. He is expecting an angry call from Fretwell in the next couple of minutes. It might be better for his credibility to get in first. He punches out the number and waits while the call rings out.

'Where the fuck is it?' Fretwell asks, the moment he answers.

'We have some problems this end, I'm afraid,' Hamilton responds. 'The senior officer in charge has signed off on the helicopter, but we're having trouble arranging a flight to Brazil from Manchester.'

'What a load of bollocks,' Fretwell says. 'I've seen on my phone that there is a flight from Manchester via Madrid to Rio at 8.15.'

Hamilton is slightly blindsided by this piece of initiative. The ability of these two men squashed into the tiniest of spaces to be able to second-guess what is being told to them about the outside world changes the dynamics entirely. The early sieges that he had been involved with, especially abroad, he could rely on having a monopoly of information from the outside world. He now has to think on his feet.

'We have to get you a private jet, don't we? We can hardly have you sharing a jumbo jet with a whole load of ordinary passengers.'

'You're just stringing us along,' Fretwell says. 'I'm not fucking stupid you know? You're going to try to wear us out to make us tired. And hope we give up. But I'll tell you this. You won't take me alive. Live free or die, that's me.'

'My job is just to end this peacefully,' Hamilton says. 'This is probably my last job, at least for this bloody lot.'

'I couldn't work with the pigs. No way.'

'I've had enough of the bureaucracy and the hassle. It wears you out, believe me.'

'So how many shooters have they got on us?' Fretwell makes it sound an innocent question, and it catches Hamilton by surprise. He lowers his voice to a bare whisper. 'Seventeen.' It is a lie. They only have 12, but it doesn't matter. It is the growing complicity that excites him. Hamilton sends a quick screen-top message, a single exclamation mark, to Alison Courtney to let her know.

'How many they got on our level?' Fretwell breathes.

Hamilton wheezes a soft chuckle. 'Can't get anyone on your floor, not outside the stairwell, not without you seeing. That little caper of moving the van really upset the bigwigs.' His slight snigger brings a matching response from Fretwell. Hamilton looks up and sees that Fynn is eyeing him as if he really is going over to the other side. He winks at the gold commander, then carries on whispering to Fretwell. 'I'll let you know if they do try to get a shooter near you. But I need you to help me. Let the child go.'

'Can't do that.'

'Think of all that crying you won't have to put up with.'

'Can't do it.'

'Bit of quiet will help all, won't it? It's a long night ahead otherwise. Let the tot go.'

'Won't do it, sorry.'

The last word, the thread of alliance between them tightening, persuades Hamilton to risk going the last inch on this tightrope.

'Come on, Liam,' Hamilton's sotto voce cadence aims for the casual entreaty of a cellmate, cadging some snout for a roll-up. 'Help us out here. I've got all these senior police chiefs scuttling about with itchy trigger fingers, wanting results, dying to come and get you.'

'Bring it on, bruv. We're fucking ready, anytime.'

'I know you are.' Hamilton lets a long and exhausted sigh blow down the line. 'God, this is like being inside again, you know?'

'So where were you banged up?'

'In the Central African Republic. A kangaroo court, my lawyer wasn't even allowed in. I couldn't understand the charges, there was just this prosecutor shouting at me and pointing his finger, and the judge was nodding his head all the time. I knew the moment they arrested me that I would be put inside.'

'What were you doing there, you stupid arsehole?' Fretwell laughs. 'You can't trust them can you? None of them down there.'

'I was working for a private security company, trying to safeguard some South African mining executives. Wasn't very successful. They were both in the next cell.'

Fretwell laughs again.

'Their company bought their freedom after a week. But I think they forgot about me. I was there for months. Where was it you did time?' He knows the answer but wants to draw Fretwell in.

'HMP Wakefield. Fucking dump run by sadists.'

'I know it. Some real hard men there.'

'Yeah.'

'At least you had decent food. The standard fare in the Bangui Hilton, as we called it, was a plate of manioc. Like eating wallpaper paste. The guards liked to mime what they had put in it too. I'm sure you can imagine. So when I say the food was shit, I literally know what I'm talking about.'

'Disgusting,' Fretwell says.

Hamilton glances sideways through the soundproof glass which connects to the rest of the command vehicle. A grinning Alison Courtney, listening in, holds both thumbs up. He winks at her. 'To be honest with you, Liam, there's not much intelligence amongst the plods out here. The bureaucracy involved in trying to get you and Jazz safely away is staggering. So many senior cops have to sign off on it. But I will continue to work away at it.'

'Doesn't surprise me to hear you are surrounded by morons.' There is the click of Fretwell's lighter and a subsequent inhalation. 'The filth were always stupid. We ran rings round them.' He laughs, then coughs. 'Who'd be a copper anyway?'

'Not me,' Hamilton chuckles. 'I had enough of uniforms when I was in Two Para. Being told what to do. The only time I really understood what I was there for was in the Falklands.' Through the glass he can see Fynn, Courtney and Gibson looking at him with approval.

'I could do with a drink,' Fretwell says. 'A proper drink.'

'You're a vodka man, aren't you? Tell you what,' Hamilton says sotto voce. 'I'm not supposed to do this, but I can get you a small bottle passed if you want. While the chief's away.'

Fretwell pauses. 'Can you make it Grey Goose, mate?'

'Give you an inch, and you take a mile!' he laughs. 'I'll try. Send Catherine to fetch it. Usual place. Give me five minutes, okay?'

'Make sure the seal's intact,' Fretwell says. 'Don't take me for a muppet, okay?'

'Absolutely. Right, got to go. But in exchange, do consider letting the child go, eh?' Hamilton hangs up.

'That was fantastic,' Courtney says. 'He's really beginning to trust you.'

'Let's hope so.'

While Fretwell is on the phone, Hoddle gets the go-ahead for Betty. He pushes the left control levers forward, and she turns sharp right, crawling steadily up the ramp. The van gradually comes into view through the ambient light micro-camera. It is parked next to the central wall, within five yards of the pedestrian stairs, lights on full beam. Betty has run up in the shadows, but for the final few yards has to cross an area of better illumination. The infrared camera shows a slight yellowish haze above and below the body of the van, but nothing through the driver's side window. This seems to indicate that both captors are in the body of the van. Now speed is of the essence. Hoddle pushes both levers to maximum, and presses the boost button. The rear propellers accelerate the vehicle to a fast walk, it quickly crosses open ground and slides underneath the middle of the van. He reverts to crawl control, and pivots the camera to inspect the underside of the Transit. His main objective is to get sight of the narrow blind spot between the van and the car park wall, and to spot any passenger side door activity. The microphone picks up conversation above, a man's voice that Hoddle presumes belongs to Fretwell.

It is now nine o'clock and the siege is three hours long. Catherine watches Fretwell on the phone. This is the most relaxed he has been. It helps that Ethan has been sleeping surprisingly well for the last half an hour, resting on her lap, with Lugs in his arm and his small pink mouth slightly open, his thumb resting on his bottom lip. She is more worried about Cousins, who has drunk two cans of Red Bull, and has gone from sleepiness right through to frenetic anxiety. He pulls a phone from his jacket pocket and begins to play with it. It is some kind of game which involved lots of beeps, and maniacal canned laughter. She had not realised that Cousins had a phone, but now he is glued to it.

She looks at her watch. Time is really dragging, each minute dotted with anxiety which just wears her out. These moments with nothing really happening inevitably lead her mind to imagining a final shootout in which she and Ethan are killed. Looking at these two she can't imagine it finishing in any other way. And part of her wants to get it over with. She looks down at her son, her precious gift to the world, and wonders what more she can do to save his life than she is already doing. Whoever it is in the police that is speaking to Fretwell seems to be doing a tremendous job. Her captors are almost animated, and Fretwell's usually stony face is revealing feelings of some kind. He seems largely immune to Ethan, which hardly anybody normal is. But there are some things Fretwell cares about, that is clear. She just hopes she and Ethan can make it, even temporarily, onto that very short list.

Fretwell ends the call and turns to Catherine. 'Got a special mission for you,' he says with something approaching a grin. 'There is a package for me on the stairs. When I give the word, you have one minute to get it and bring it back to me.'

'What's going on?' Cousins asks.

'We're getting some vodka, from the chief constable's personal stash probably.'

'What for?'

'Don't you worry about it. It's for me. There is some squaddie working with the filth, and he's given me some of the inside info. He clearly can't stand them.'

'What are you doing, Fretty?' Cousins demands. 'They have hostage negotiators whose job is to make you lower your guard. And it's happening.'

'Fuck off,' Fretwell says, lighting up another cigarette. 'I've got it all under control.' He carefully peers through the van's front windows. 'They think I've been taken in, but I haven't.' He eases open the driver's door, runs around the back, pulls open the rear door and brings Catherine out.

He doesn't know that just 20 yards away, lying under a car, someone has the back of his head in a telescopic sight.

Chapter Eleven

Samira Dev is cradling her sniper's rifle carefully with the sight against her right eye. Her breathing is even and slow. She is in the shadows under a parked Skoda Fabia; her slender 5-foot-1-inch frame makes her the only candidate in the firearms unit able to squeeze under this smallish car. And it had to be this car because it is the only one which gives a good view of the Transit's rear doors. Though there are perhaps a dozen other vehicles on this floor, most are clustered at the other end, in front of the van and by the pedestrian exit. No one could reach them without it being obvious to anyone sitting in the front seats of the Transit.

It is her first live assignment.

Dev had not had it easy trying to get into a police firearms unit, despite her Commonwealth Games silver medal in shooting for Pakistan. She was too small for general recruitment into the British police. So it had taken four years, and a special dispensation under a diversity programme, for her to be considered at all. Her problems did not end at admission. The police culture remains macho and stubbornly lacking in racial diversity. So when she asked to be considered for a firearms unit placing after just 18 months in the force, her universally white male colleagues laughed. She would fail the fitness test, they said, which has to be conducted in full body armour and helmet. However, a senior intelligence officer took her aside at interview. Her application mentioned that she spoke fluent Urdu and some Arabic. After briefly trying to persuade her to become a counter-terrorism intelligence officer, he agreed that her linguistic understanding would be a tremendous asset as a firearms officer in many terrorism scenarios. She did indeed struggle with the fitness regime while wearing body armour, but she came top in every single shooting competition. In the end they could not deny her.

After being dropped by helicopter with three other firearms officers onto the open top level of the car park, she had made her way down with PC Wayne Haskins to the level immediately above the hostage vehicle. Under cover of overhead helicopter noise they were able to access the half floor which gave a partial view of the van. Haskins, a beefy 6 feet 2 inches, was too big a target to risk crossing the open ramp to get close to the Skoda. Even looking in the van's wing mirror, he would be obvious. But Samira Dev was another matter. While Hamilton had been chatting to Fretwell, she slipped across without being seen. Crouching down behind the Skoda, she realised that she could not fit beneath with her helmet on. She considered it a risk worth taking. After a full minute of wriggling and crawling, she got the tip of her rifle just three inches short of the left-hand sill, with a good view down the ramp to the rear of the Transit.

And now Liam Fretwell, the convicted murderer considered to be the most dangerous of the two hostage takers, is within easy range. She whispers into her mic that she has him in her sight and asks: 'Anyone else got a bead on Cousins?'

For an agonising ten seconds there is no reply, enough time for Fretwell to gain the back of the van and open the door. For a further few seconds he is hidden from view behind the Transit's rear door. No one has a good angle on Cousins. She hears Fynn's laconic voice urging calm.

She watches as the woman she has seen before is pulled roughly out of the van. 'Female hostage clear, over.'

Catherine runs to the pedestrian exit, pulls open the door and enters the landing. Where there was previously a package of food, there is now a small bottle of vodka resting on a piece of paper. She sets aside her curiosity that the police seem to be supplying spirits to her captors and instead reads the message written beneath.

> WE CAN NOW HEAR CONVERSATION INSIDE THE VAN. IF YOU FEEL THAT YOUR LIFE OR THAT OF YOUR CHILD IS IN IMMINENT DANGER SHOUT THE CODEWORD:
>
> JUPITER.
>
> THAT WILL TRIGGER OUR INTERVENTION. DESTROY THIS MESSAGE AND DO NOT MENTION IT.

While Catherine is running to the landing, Fretwell has other tasks to accomplish. Cousins gives him a small ziplock bag containing two small yellow tablets, and he crushes them carefully under his heel, making a gritty dust. He takes one of the small yoghurt pots which he has hidden in the front of the van, peels the foil lid back a little and pours in some of the powdered pills. Using his little finger he stirs the yoghurt.

'You're not going to try and feed it are you?' Cousins asks.

'Nah, she can do that when she gets back innit?' he grins. He attempts to reseal the lid and puts the yoghurt back in the glove compartment.

Catherine comes back with the bag and offers it to Fretwell. 'It's vodka,' she says, nodding at the bottle. 'Seems you have made a friend.'

'Yeah well, don't count on it,' he replies, quietly and then adds: 'So how many cops did you see in the stairwell?'

The question catches her off balance because she hadn't been asked last time. She hesitates, and then realises that is absolutely the wrong thing to do.

'So you definitely saw some?' Cousins asks.

'Yes, there are lots. With guns and all sorts of stuff.'

'What did they say to you?' Fretwell asks.

'Nothing.'

'Don't you bloody lie to me, bitch! Course they're going to try to pass a message to you. I'm not stupid, so don't you take me for an idiot.' Fretwell pulls out the knife which has not been seen for nearly two hours. He lunges across the back of the van and seizes Catherine's face between his fingers 'Do you remember what this can do?' He holds the bloodstained tip of the blade close to her eye.

Catherine can't help but whimper a little. 'You're hurting me.' The disturbance has woken Ethan up, who is now grizzling.

Fretwell laughs. 'Of course I'm hurting you. I mean to hurt you, I like to hurt you, I enjoy hurting you. Get it?'

Catherine attempts to nod her head, but she is held too rigidly to do that, so she signals her acquiescence by closing her eyes. 'But if you hurt me, you'll make Ethan cry. I've been trying to stop him crying. We all have.'

Fretwell snorts. 'But it's your lucky day ain't it? I found you a yoghurt for the sprog.' He lets go of her face, slides over the passenger seat and reaches to the glove compartment. He then pulls out the yoghurt, slithers back and offers it to her.

Catherine takes the yoghurt and eyes it suspiciously. 'It's been opened.'

'So?' He looks at Cousins and rolls his eyes. 'No fucking gratitude, eh? Jesus Christ.'

'Well, I suppose I should say thank you.' She looks up at him and wonders if it is from the food parcel. Perhaps he has the rest of the yoghurts too. She doesn't dare to ask him, but it is still an encouraging sign. 'There was a plastic spoon in the bag originally.' She looks at Fretwell's tightening face and hurriedly adds: 'Well never mind, it would have made it a bit easier. But I can feed him from my finger.'

'Just keep him quiet, all right?'

Cousins is examining the vodka. It's a premium Grey Goose and the seal is intact. He twists the cap, and holds the bottle to his nose. 'It's the real thing.' He sounds surprised.

'Yeah well, hand it over, it's mine,' Fretwell says. Cousins passes the bottle across and Fretwell takes a pull on it. They both watch as Catherine dips a finger into the yoghurt and lifts some out. But Ethan isn't playing ball. He's lying against Catherine's leg, eyes tightly shut and screeching. She strokes his head, and makes gentle shushing sounds, but this only seems to stir him to a greater squall.

'Come on little man,' Catherine says, with a note of urgency in her voice. She is aware of the muttering and complaining made by the captors about the increased noise levels. 'Have some yoghurt, it's banana.' She brings her yoghurt laden finger close to Ethan's mouth but he pushes it away without even looking and starts screeching louder still.

'Jesus Christ,' Fretwell exclaims. 'You promised you'd keep him shut up. We get you a fucking yoghurt, but you still can't do the job, can you?'

'He's tired, he's disturbed by the noises, all the cigarette smoke, and by the anxiety he senses in me. Babies are sensitive creatures, they know what is going on around them and they react.' She looks at Fretwell, daring to make eye contact. 'If you go a bit easier on me, then he will settle.'

As if by magic, Ethan suddenly stops crying, opens his eyes and looks at his mother. He takes several big shuddering breaths. As she lifts him up into the crook of her arm, she again offers him the remains of the yoghurt on her finger. But as Ethan parts his lips, she suddenly looks down. 'There's grit or something in this,' she says.

'I'm sure it's fine,' says Fretwell.

Catherine senses something is not right. Her captors seem to have nothing better to do than watch her feed Ethan. Her gut instinct is signalling that something is very wrong. The captors have for the last few hours been almost immune to Ethan. But now they almost seem to be holding their breath as they watch her feed our child. The realisation comes to her in a flash. The grit is from some kind of tablet. They're attempting to drug him, presumably to keep him quiet. But she has no idea what they have used. If they are drug dealers it could be anything toxic, dangerous and at the very least unsuitable for a young baby. The question now is what to do about it. She returns the yoghurt to its pot by wiping her finger on the rim. 'No, I think we'll give it a miss.'

At that moment Ethan, looking at the yoghurt, decides to contest his mother's judgement with a renewed bout of crying. Fretwell and Cousins look at each other with exasperation, so Catherine asks: 'Do you have another yoghurt, with the seal intact?'

'No, we bloody well ain't.' Fretwell's face is tightening even more as Ethan's distress turns into a heartfelt wail. 'So give him that.'

Catherine picks Ethan up, and croons gently into his ear as she jiggles him about trying to stop his crying. She watches as the coiled spring that is Fretwell tightens and tightens. Something horrible is going to happen if Ethan doesn't be quiet, but she is at her wits' end to know what to do. Cousins is knocker watching again, but is otherwise saying little. She checks Ethan's nappy, which is fine, and then decides to try to breastfeed him again. She turns away from Cousins, lifts her blouse, but Ethan will not take her nipple and instead cries anew.

Fretwell is close to boiling, and kicks hard against the side of the van, cursing repeatedly and then shouts: 'I'm going to kill him, if he doesn't shut up I promise I'm going to kill him.'

Catherine barely has time to speak before she sees the knife, and Fretwell's lightning fast movement towards her across the van.

Chapter Twelve

PC Alison Courtney holds her headphones tight to her ears. Hamilton is leaning over her shoulder and asks her to put the microphone on public so they can all hear it. The sounds are sibilant, metallic and peppered with the rumble of lower register interference, but the basic theme is obvious. The baby is crying, and the hostage takers are once again threatening Catherine Blake.

'Has anyone got a clear line on either of the targets?' Fynn barks into the radio. All that comes back are breathy bursts of static, and then the word negative, from one shooter after another.

Fynn sighs, and puts the handset down. He looks up at Hamilton. 'Any ideas?'

'I've been expecting a call from Fretwell about the non-appearance of the chopper,' Hamilton says. 'But he probably can't hear himself think with the baby crying.'

'Ethan's noise might wear them all even faster than would normally happen in a siege,' Courtney says.

'I'm sure,' Hamilton concedes. 'But then they might just kill him. They will still have one hostage, and they might think they are in a more predictable situation.'

'I don't agree with that calculus,' Fynn says. 'If they are thinking straight, they will know that murdering a baby will bring us down on them like a ton of bricks.'

'Who said either of them are thinking straight?' interjects Courtney.

'Fretwell will go down fighting,' Hamilton says. 'Everything I've read about him says so. Three dead already, including a female police officer. They've nothing to lose now.'

'You may be out of date on the body count,' Gibson says, pointing at his screen. 'A woman has been reported dead late this afternoon outside the flat where Fretwell used to live, and just a dozen yards from where the husband of Mrs Blake was killed.'

'Any details?' Fynn asks.

'Head injuries,' Gibson said. 'It was initially assumed to be an accident, as she was at the bottom of a flight of stairs. We'll not know for a while. There's also another report, so far unconfirmed, of the body of a disabled man found in Levenshulme, not far off the known path of the vehicle.'

'Jesus Christ,' Fynn says. 'At least we've got these animals penned up now.'

'But look who's stuck in the cage with them,' Courtney adds.

That comment silences them all. Hamilton peers at his watch. It's nearly ten. The siege has now been going on for nearly four hours.

Fynn looks at each of them in turn. 'Everybody's doing a great job, and I know it sounds like mayhem in there, but I'm committed to at least trying to drag the current status quo on until the small hours. We will replace the stairwell, roof and remote observation teams at midnight. I don't think we can do that with our forward sharpshooter, it's too dangerous to get her out. I'll be staying for the duration, but I'll see if we can get you both relieved by two a.m.'

Alison Courtney interrupts. 'Sir, there's something happening. Movement in the van, and screaming.'

Catherine flinches as Fretwell approaches with the knife, but it isn't her or the child that is the target. Instead he grabs Lugs from Ethan's grasp, and retreats with the stuffed rabbit to the other side of the van. Ethan squirms around to see what has happened, and sees his beloved companion in the hands of the man who had hurt his mother. His face crumples in alarm and despondency.

'Hey Ethan, look,' Fretwell says with a malicious grin scrawled across his face. He waggles Lugs backwards and forwards. And then he brings the knife up to the rabbit's neck. 'If you don't shut up, you know what's going to happen next.'

'He doesn't understand,' Catherine pleads. 'Don't play with him like that, it will only make things worse.' Right on cue Ethan's crying intensifies.

'Who's fucking playing?' Fretwell says, and plunges the knife right through the stuffed animal. Ethan's reaction is immediate and heartbreaking. His howls of anguish and terror outdo anything that he has produced so far.

'SHUT UP, you little wanker.' Fretwell rips the animal to pieces, pulling out the stuffing, and running the blade through the rabbit time and again.

Catherine is barely able to make herself heard above her son, but the symbolism of Fretwell's cruelty makes her blood run cold. She feels the moment approaching when she will have to sacrifice her life to stop this madman.

But it is Cousins who intercedes first. 'Fretty, did you have to do that?' he shouts. 'You've just made it worse.'

'Lugs is as real to Ethan as you or I,' Catherine says. 'He's his best friend and has comforted him every night and every day since his birth. That is a terrible, terrible thing you have done.'

'Yeah, Fretty, it's a murder.'

'Well, I'm a murderer. What do you fucking expect?' he laughs, and takes a long draw on the Grey Goose.

For the next ten minutes Ethan wails and sobs and will not be comforted by anything Catherine does. She recalls the worst nights when he was teething, now some months ago, when she woke up in the morning unsure whether she had slept at all. She hadn't thought anything could be worse than that. But now she is learning how wrong she was.

Paddy Hamilton listens in to the mayhem inside the van. 'Thank God we can still hear the voice of Catherine and her child.'

'But what are they doing to them?' Courtney asks.

'I think we can safely say that it is hell in there,' Fynn says.

'Not hellish enough for Mrs Blake to use the panic word,' Gibson says.

'She knows that would be a last-ditch defence. Unfortunately it is more than forty-five minutes since we had either of these bastards in our crosshairs. And until we get a clear shot at both I am not sanctioning an intervention,' Fynn says.

The others nod in agreement. It is nearly midnight. Over the next 15 minutes the sound levels within the van start to decline. There seems less physical movement, which gets picked up as metallic noises on the two mics, one on Betty underneath the van, the other suspended over the parapet from the floor above. There is some conversation, but the baby no longer seems to be crying. A buzz of radio static prefaces a call from Samira Dev. 'Got a clear target on Cousins. He's just emerged from the van.'

'Is he armed?' Fynn asks.

'Not that I can see. Over.'

'What's he doing?'

'He's moved twenty yards or so along the inner wall. Now he's crouching down.' There is a long pause and a slight ripple of laughter. 'He's unbuckled his belt...'

'All right, Dev, I think we know what is happening. Over.' Fynn looks around the command van. 'This should be an opportunity, don't you think Alison?'

'He's a rapist, so can we get her to shoot him in the balls?' she mutters.

'Tempting, but we don't know what effect that would have on Fretwell, do we?' Hamilton says.

They are interrupted by a call which Fynn takes on his own mobile. The others notice a certain stiffening in the commander's bearing as he begins to talk. 'Yes, absolutely. No,

I think we've got everything we need.' When the two-minute call finishes he turns to face Hamilton. 'The Home Secretary. She expressed a desire to see a peaceful resolution.'

'And so say all of us,' Hamilton mutters.

'Cousins appears to be back in the van,' Courtney says.

The monitored phone rings. 'That will be Fretwell,' Hamilton says, hurrying back to the booth to take it.

Fretwell has the Grey Goose in one hand and his mobile in the other. 'Right, mate, so you lied to me about the chopper.'

'I didn't lie. They told me yes, now someone higher up has told me no. So we have to deal with it. It would certainly help my case with them if you would give up one of the hostages, the child, as a mark of good faith.'

Fretwell doesn't say anything for a long time. Catherine hasn't seen any evidence that he is drunk, but he certainly seems less on edge now than he had been. Perhaps he accepts the inevitability of his own capture. Or perhaps it is the inevitability of death.

'No way. Absolutely no way.' Fretwell removes the handgun from his waistband and examines it, checking the clip for ammunition and miming shots at Catherine, Ethan and Cousins. 'The only reason you've not stormed the van is because we've got them both, he's helpless and she's useless.' Fretwell glances at the child.

Ethan has cried himself out and is lying asleep in Catherine's lap. She has had to change him again, and did it quickly and efficiently this time. She is dog tired too, and wants to sleep more than anything in the world. My poor, lonely wife is thinking of me, but there is nothing I can do to help her. She doesn't want to fall asleep. She is terrified that if she does she would forget that I am dead, and would suffer upon waking the shock and the grief all over again.

'Well Liam, there is some chance of a deal tomorrow morning, but for tonight that is it. We'll be keeping an eye on you and hoping that when you had a chance to sleep on it you'll have changed your mind.'

Fretwell hangs up angrily, swearing at the phone. He lights up a cigarette, and sucks deeply on it before blowing a huge plume of smoke up towards the ceiling. 'Well Jazz, looks like we're stuck here just waiting for them to decide that they are going to come in guns blazing.'

Cousins, who has returned from his toilet break more anxious than ever, is playing with his phone again. He looks across to Fretwell. 'I told you we should never have brought them with us,' he says, inclining his head towards Catherine and Ethan. 'I knew it was trouble.'

'You've been fuck-all help from the start. So don't you start on me, all right?' Fretwell takes a swig of the vodka, and follows it with a gulp of Red Bull. 'We don't have to wait for the filth to give you the bullet. I could do it now.'

The expanding hostility between the two offers Catherine renewed hope but also raises new fears. She watches as discreetly as she can as Fretwell plays with the gun and berates Cousins. The younger man doesn't make eye contact, but returns to his phone, and the irritating whoosh and jingle of the game. Cousins' toes are flexing inside his trainers, the only sign that Catherine can see of the fidgety, fearful mood he is in. Fretwell scowls at him with undisguised loathing.

I know that my clever wife is working out where the two weapons are and if she has a chance of seizing the gun.

The interior light of the van seems to be dimming. Catherine isn't sure whether the darkness outside is contributing, or the police have turned down the ceiling lights in the car park. Fretwell too is staring up at the white plastic light housing. His conclusion is simple. 'Van battery's fucked. Stupid arsehole couldn't even look after something that simple.'

She isn't immediately aware who is the target of this invective. Then it dawns on her that the van's previous owner, who paid with his life for being in the wrong place at the wrong time, is having insult added to terminal injury.

'You shouldn't have left the headlights on for the last three hours,' Cousins says, without even looking up from his game.

'Fuck off. How are we supposed to see if the filth come piling out of the stairwell then, you moron?' Fretwell curses his co-conspirator, and slithers over into the driving seat. He turns the ignition key and presses the accelerator. The van starter motor wheezes, like a slow laugh, but the engine doesn't fire. He tries twice more, cursing inventively at the van as if it is somehow responsible for this lethargy. 'Useless fucking thing!' He pulls out the knife and stabs at the dashboard in frustration. He scores across the leatherette backwards and forwards, the tip of the blade grinding into the metal beneath.

Catherine is amazed. The entire world, the living and the inanimate, are in Fretwell's view conspiring against him, frustrating his desires. She has been gradually trying to understand what makes him tick, to work out weaknesses and vulnerabilities that she can somehow exploit. The inner strength which I saw in her over the months and years of IVF, of pain and disappointment, is now being deployed in a similarly slow-burning cause. There is a single mindedness about my lovely wife that I hope will sustain her even in the darkest moments.

Fretwell, having given up trying to start the engine, turns off the headlight and slithers back into the main compartment. He looks up at the interior light and says: 'This should hold up a bit longer now.'

'Yeah maybe,' Cousins says, still engrossed in his phone, thumbs busy.

Catherine stares up at the rectangular fixture, from which the light has faded from a harsh white to a soft caramel over the last hour. The glow from Cousins' phone, which bathes the bottom of his face in a Mephistophelean hue, is now the dominant source of illumination. The man is still a source of mystery to Catherine. While she feels she has a grip on the tantrum-fed persona of Fretwell, the still waters of Cousins' evil remain unfathomable. In the encroaching gloom of the metal box, the walls seem to shrink in, the confinement gathering in intensity. Catherine is sitting with her legs tucked up towards her chin, Ethan sleeping beatifically at her side, cuddled around the curve of her hip, a thumb in his mouth. In his other hand he clenches a torn remnant of Lugs, now little more than a grease-slicked shred of fleece and a puff of nylon stuffing.

Cousins' long legs reach out on either side of Catherine like the jaws of a crocodile, grazing her thigh on the left, and almost touching Ethan on the right. Fretwell by contrast is almost a blur of nervous movements, his right leg extended along the back edge of the driving compartment, and his foot tapping to a fast and unseen rhythm. His left leg is folded up with his knee towards his chin, and he's working away with his knife, fraying the knee on his newly acquired joggers. He is smoking another cigarette, and seems to be almost halfway down the bottle of Grey Goose. If he is drunk, there is no outward sign.

Catherine clears her throat. 'I want to tell you about my husband.'

Cousins looks up and eyes her quizzically.

But it is Fretwell who speaks first. 'No fucking point is there?'

'He was a good man, a good father. He did everything...'

'Save it for the headstone.' Fretwell is back on the phone, flicking through videos on YouTube. 'If the wanker hadn't tried to stop us, he would still be alive. Simple.'

'He was trying to save us.'

Fretwell scoffed. 'He hadn't a chance.'

Reluctantly, Catherine has to agree with him. 'So is there anything that you care about?'

Fretwell takes another swig of the vodka. 'Nah.' His eyes lose a little focus, as he stares up at the failing light. 'It's dog eat dog innit?'

Cousins adds his own comment: 'He cares about Man U.'

Fretwell cuts across him. 'You spend time in Wakefield, you see how it is. A fucking jungle.' He starts flicking through videos. 'People like you, in the nine-to-five, not a clue. But you still get shafted, dontcha? Redundancy, pay cuts. Same shit.'

Catherine looks at him, the first thread glimpsed in his philosophy.

Fretwell is still thumbing up through videos. 'My brother, grafter, right? Come to see me in Wakefield, couple of years ago. Surprised, really. First time since I'd been put away. Told me this story. Worked eight weeks on this big house in Alderley Edge. Massive fucking kitchen he put in there. At the end, the geezer didn't want to pay. Some fat businessman. Forty-six grand, my brother was out of pocket. Took him to court.' He paused. 'Waste of time. Rigged innit?'

Fretwell eyes Catherine, something almost like pain in those azure eyes. 'I listened and then at the end there was this big silence. I let it sit there like a big fat turd on the carpet. Then he looks down at his hands and says: "You've got friends outside. Can you do something about it, Liam?" That's what he says.'

Catherine listens to him in silence. Fretwell is now working away with his knife on the lining of the back of the seats, carving off small pieces of the vinyl. His outstretched leg is jiggling away with nervous energy.

'Seven fucking years, not a peep. Now this. He must have thought I was a fucking muppet.' He looks at Catherine, and at Ethan, as if he is warning the child. 'Everybody wants something.'

'Did you help him?' Catherine asks.

Fretwell grins, an evil smile, and looks at Cousins. 'Fucking did. Tell her, Jazz.'

'I burnt it down,' Cousins says. 'While they were on holiday.'

'Whole fucking house, kitchen, conservatory, indoor fucking sauna, the lot.' Fretwell is enjoying the tale.

'Is that what your brother wanted?' Catherine asks.

Fretwell looked at her as if she was stupid. 'Nah. Especially when the filth pulled him in for five hours questioning. He might have forgotten that his little brother was banged up. But the coppers hadn't. They talked about nothing else. And they knew he'd been to see me.'

'Did he come and see you again?' Catherine asks.

The leg was going nineteen to the dozen now. 'Nah.'

Outside the car park the streets are thronged with onlookers, all staring up at what had been until today the most forgettable concrete structure in the area. Although it is one in the morning, Manchester's late-night revellers have found something just as interesting as nightclubbing. A mobile burger van is doing a roaring trade, not only because of the hundreds of sightseers but also from the police. Behind the crowd barriers, looking up, is the leader of the Moss Side Mafia. Nathaniel Raymond Blades, mixed race, 34 years old, 5 feet 9, well-built but not enough to attract attention, brown eyes, shaven headed and normally with a sizeable black beard. Unusually, Blades sports no visible tattoos, and hasn't done a day of prison time since his early 20s. Which isn't to say he isn't breaking the law on a regular basis. Blades, inevitably known as Ray-Zer, is one of the cleverest criminals in the city, a man adept at getting others to do the dirty work that keeps his gang the most feared on the streets.

Today he is wearing a smart charcoal-grey overcoat, a traditional cloth cap and tiny sunglasses. His beard is dyed blond, and worn Viking style in two short plaits. He is staring up at that car park with an intensity that would bore holes in it.

Blades has a little empire. Across the metropolis, he owns a small chain of betting shops, a tattoo parlour, a pizza joint and a small garage. None of them seem to make much money, after the expenses, the cars and staff wages. CID is convinced that the proceeds of the Moss Side Mafia's amphetamine trade are laundered through these other businesses. But proving it is turning out to be very difficult. The betting shops, particularly, with a huge intake of cash bets, are proving hard to pin down. There are clearly some astute but bent accountants involved.

Why is my restless spirit drawn to Blades? Quite simply because as the head of the gang, Nathaniel Blades might be the only person able to order Fretwell to let my wife and child go free.

If he can be persuaded to do it.

The light inside the van is almost gone, leaving only the blue-tinted illumination from mobile phones. Fretwell and Cousins are separately busy with their thumbs. From the sounds she hears, and the slight grin on his face, Catherine believes Fretwell is looking at video clips of Manchester United. By contrast

Cousins is now much quieter, concentrating on something on his screen. He hasn't looked up in quite a while. She checks her wristwatch. 1.20 a.m. She is dog tired, and despite the open driver's side window, Fretwell's chain-smoking is beginning to suffocate her. She is amazed that Ethan is able to sleep through it all.

'Can we have the rear door open a crack? The smoke is really bothering me,' she says.

The reply is a predictable volley of Fs and Cs from Fretwell. 'I wasn't born yesterday,' he adds. She thinks ruefully about Ethan, who pretty much was born yesterday, and the effect on his tiny lungs of this exposure. But then she catches herself. Thoughts like that belong to another life, when what might happen in years or decades was worth considering. Just getting through the night alive is all that is important now.

Cousins seems to be doing something serious on the phone, as his demeanour has changed. He has almost imperceptibly angled the screen away from Fretwell, and his right shoulder has edged forward to guard what it is he is working on. An incoming text flashes onto the screen. Catherine herself is pretty good at reading upside down, What she sees amazes her.

Cousins stops for a moment, then his thumbs are a blur, and she can't see what he has replied. But now at least she knows that two sides are forming in this siege. And she has to decide quickly which one is best for her and for Ethan. The end may come soon now, one way or another. She kisses Ethan's head, just in case she doesn't ever have the chance to do it again.

Chapter Thirteen

Blades has stayed back from the front of the crowd but has still been recognised. A middle-aged female cop is pretending not to look at him. But the body language is a giveaway. There's a bit of silver bling on her uniform, so she could be senior. Nothing to worry about, he tells himself. Unlike up there.

Fretwell. What a piece of work. He's always been a loose cannon, with an unpredictable temper and a shortage of grey matter. Blades was reluctant to cut him and Cousins loose, but it was fuck-up after high-profile fuck-up. Getting Sparko Sinclair, fine. He knew where the money and gear was. But killing Lorraine Caldwell, what was that about? She had been a useful informant. Now the cops. One dead, one critically injured, and finally this stupid hostage drama. The wrath of Greater Manchester Police was on them, big time. The cops had raided his mum's house, the flats of two gang members, and had made half a dozen targeted stop and searches since this afternoon.

At eight o'clock he'd gone round to see his mum, who was upset. She said the cops had made a mess, but hadn't apparently found anything, except a phone belonging to him. 'Tell Blades to look after his stuff,' is what she had been told.

But they had left the phone behind. That was very odd.

Blades was puzzled. He looked at the mobile, which was on the lounge table. It wasn't his, and he told her. While they were both looking at it, it rang. Blades indicated his mother should answer it. She did, and her eyes immediately flicked up to her son. 'It's the police, for you.'

He groaned. 'Mum, for Christ's sake, don't tell them I'm here.'

'I think they know.' She nodded towards the window. A dark car was parked opposite, a hand waving from the window in greeting.

Blades took the phone warily. It was a detective who he had known years ago, a local guy who knew the gang as well as anyone. 'Got a message for you from on high,' the cop said. 'We know you've been in contact with 'em. Use your influence to end the siege peacefully. If anyone else dies we are coming in like fucking Daleks to exterminate the Moss Side Mafia. HMRC will raid your betting shops, health and safety will close down your tattoo parlour, your car repair place will be shafted under trading standards, everything. The road will be dug up right outside your pizza joint, and not filled in again until it's gone bust. We can play dirty too. You'll not have a moment's peace. On the other hand, give us Fretwell, and we may cut you some slack. Think about it.'

The line was cut.

Blades had only ever had one similar contact from the police. That was a couple of years ago when one of the gang's handguns had turned up in the hands of a jihadi from Oldham. The police line was: we know you have shooters, do not ever, ever pass them to terrorists, or the sky will fall in on you.

So what to do? The gang had dealt with members who had gone freelance before. Payments could be docked, wrists could be broken, faces could be marked for ever. Fretwell has been useful, over the years. But all good things come to an end. Everyone in B wing at Wakefield said Fretwell had gone radio rentals. Seeming to be mental just to scare people was one thing, but losing your nous, well, that's another. Blades had always told them that knowing how to hide your money *before* you grab it is crucial, but Fretwell obviously hadn't listened. When it came to the loot from RHC22, he was almost caught red-handed with it in his own flat by the police. But to panic and hand it to a neighbour, a drunken loser like Sparko Sinclair, that was stupid. This is a business and judgement is everything. Now Fretwell had compounded the problem by leaving a trail of bodies in an attempt to get the money and gear back. No wonder the cops were like a stirred-up red ants' nest.

It isn't a hard decision to make. Blades types out a few fateful characters and sends the message. Less than a minute after his message to Cousins, a reply comes back:

OK. Then what?

Catherine is trying to read the phone again without making it obvious. Her eyes are half closed to disguise this intention, and she is running her fingers through her blood-matted hair. It's a painful business, as coppery threads are stuck to her ear and freeing them may cause the wound to reopen. She works methodically, freeing one hair at a time. But she has glanced at the screen, and what she sees is both frightening and hopeful. Someone outside, an enemy of Fretwell's, seems to have authority over Cousins. The message makes that very clear.

Cousins blinks, clicks the phone off and slides it into his pocket. His eyes flick sideways towards Fretwell, still engrossed in the football videos. Catherine watches the brown-skinned man take an enormous breath, and let it out slowly. There is a brief flicker in his eyes which might indicate emotion of some kind: fear, perhaps, or excitement. The flexing of toes within his trainers has begun again too. She can't see where Fretwell is keeping the pistol, he's moved it from pocket to waistband and back again numerous times. She tries to discern whether the jacket looks weighted with it or not. She thinks not, which would mean the weapon is tucked down the back of his trousers. Sitting opposite her, Cousins is three feet or so nearer the rear doors than Fretwell, who is tucked into the corner behind the seats. Slowly, Cousins pulls his feet in, and raises himself to a crouch. Fretwell glances over at him, and then returns to his videos.

Catherine senses what is about to happen, and looks down at Ethan. Our child is fast asleep, his eyes moving slightly behind his eyelids, tiny fists almost balled. The innocence and vulnerability of this last moment in time before all hell breaks loose. She knows that the moment Cousins makes his move she will have to shout out the panic word.

Let me tell you about being dead. In the one minute before this feared climax, I had only departed this life a little over 11 hours. But in my new ethereal mode, I have been as close to my wife as it is possible to be. I don't know if it is possible for my spirit to in any way bolster hers, or if my wider visits to the surrounding police and even other gang members give her any shared inkling of what may now occur. All I know is that in a few seconds the lives of my beautiful wife and precious son will balance on a knife edge, and all the screamed but silent warnings I am trying to project appear to have had no effect whatsoever.

Except on Ethan.

My son's bright blue eyes suddenly flick open, alert and watching, as if he at least knows that something terrible is about to happen to his world, and the mother around whom it is built.

Chapter Fourteen

Janile Cousins blinks twice, exactly the same reptilian reflex Catherine has seen when he eats. She watches his mouth form an O, a deliberate slow exhalation, like the ones she has learned to make in pilates. Fretwell's consciousness seems to be confined within a phone-sized rendition of Manchester United's latest victory. He feels for the neck of the Grey Goose and lifts it to his lips.

It is the last everyday action inside the van.

Cousins leaps sideways at Fretwell, grabbing for the weapon down the back of his jeans. Fretwell swivels, shedding surprise in a millisecond, and swings the bottle at his assailant's head. It connects but doesn't break, sloshing vodka over the darker man's face. The two wrestle on the rumbling floor, screeching and growling at each other like animals. Catherine, still sitting, swivels left and grabs Ethan. She then rolls over on her back to the right, places him lying down in comparative safety by the rear door, then continues the roll until she is face down, the child tucked below her. It is exactly what she was told to do.

First priority accomplished she turns her head to look at the fight and bellows as loudly as she can:

'Jupiter!'

The only illumination is Fretwell's phone, which is skittering and jumping with every impact on the scuffed metal surface, while the cheering background of the football video gives a strange tinny applause for the struggle inside the vehicle. In the bluish light she can make out a glint from a dark metallic shape, thrumming on the floor underneath Fretwell's back. Both assailants are scrabbling for it.

The gun.

Fretwell, his own arms partially pinioned, still manages to bludgeon two or three vicious headbutts into his opponent's face. The crack of breaking bone makes Catherine's stomach turn over. Cousins springs back and to his feet, the pistol now in his hand, blood streaming from his nose. Fretwell, crouched, has the knife in his right.

'Come on then, if you want some,' Fretwell hisses.

It seems ages since Catherine gave her shout so she repeats the word: 'Jupit—'.

Before she has finished a thunderous metallic roar drowns the van, followed by the whine of ricochets.

It is 3.21 a.m. Neil Fynn is outside the van, coffee in hand when he hears a shout from inside. It is Alison Courtney: 'Sir, Jupiter!'

Courtney switches Betty's microphone so that it now broadcasts inside the command van, but the cacophony of shouting is so intense that Fynn has to jump back outside to give the command to his sharpshooters. One second later he sees the searchlights go on, and hears a fusillade crackle from at least three directions. The bystanders crouch down as deafening echoes rebound from every building in the vicinity. This is what they have come to see.

The climactic shootout.

Samira Dev has the Heckler and Koch ready on semi-automatic when the call comes. Without either hostage-taker in her sights she blasts 12 crisp horizontal shots, like rivets, along the body of the van, halfway between the top of the wheel arch and the roof. She then signals the all-clear with her left arm stuck out from under the car. From behind her PC Wayne Haskins and two other armed officers in full body armour go roaring down the ramp headed for the rear doors of the van. Dev is not particularly religious, but she prays that the hostage and child were lying down as instructed.

In the flickering light of the stairwell PC Philippa Caldicot has her headphones tuned in to the van, and so directly hears Catherine call the panic word. The ten second delay before the gold commander confirms the assault seems more like an hour, particularly as she hears the full violence of what is happening inside that vehicle. The moment she detects Fynn on the broadcast channel, she signals for PCs O'Donnell and Searle to go in. By the time the chief superintendent has given her the okay they are already down the stairs, through the door, and sprinting to the van, yelling for surrender. She follows a few seconds later.

In the brief buzzing silence there is an unearthly slurping sound. Cousins is staggering, a gory hole in the front of his throat venting breath. The gun is still in his hand, a wisp of vapour rising and the stink of propellant. Fretwell, still crouched and apparently untouched, has the knife in his right hand, and his left stretched out, fingers beckoning Cousins. 'Come on, I'm ready,' he whispers.

Cousins eyes roll back into his head, and with a final bloody wheeze he collapses next to Catherine.

'Gotcha now,' Fretwell rasps and leaps on him. The knife arm flashes across Catherine's vision towards Cousins' unprotected chest. Instinctively, she jumps for the blade, seizing Fretwell's wrist in both hands, and tipping him over onto his back.

The shouts of police and the pounding of approaching boots buoys her spirits but the strength in Fretwell's knife arm is astonishing, and exceeds that in both of hers. 'Help me, help me...' she squeals in desperation. If only she can hold him just a few seconds more.

But Fretwell is too experienced to be troubled. With lightning speed, his left arm crosses the restrained right and the blade winks out to reappear magically in his left. Somehow he is now back on his feet, and she is half underneath him. Catherine lets go of the wrist, and rolls over to shield Ethan. She senses with a grim certainty that his retaliation will be to strike at what is dearest to her.

Two more bullets bang through the windscreen and whine through the van. She feels a brief shudder in Fretwell. A wet, red flower appears by his collarbone, but he doesn't seem to notice. His narrowed eyes are lasered on her, his mean mouth in a sadistic grin.

'Teach you, bitch.' He lunges over her towards the child, and she tracks the glinting trajectory millisecond by millisecond. From her prone position, her leg shoots up, intending to somehow knock the knife from his hand. Instead the blade disappears handle-deep into her calf and is torn from his grasp. Expecting pain, she feels just cold fury and goes for him with both hands, nails clawing, growling, just as she had promised, and finds her target in the soft flesh of his face.

The van's windscreen explodes. A fusillade of bullets from close by.

The rear doors are flung open, and suddenly there are bright lights.

And a cold agony is gripping her leg.

A crowd of black-clad police are shouting, front and rear. The driver's door is torn open. There are guns from all directions. But she and the man who wants to kill her child are entangled like writhing snakes. She stares into his face, smells his fetid breath, his open mouth, gushing crimson. His knitted eyebrows turn from furious to puzzled. His eyes, the bluest of blue, ice over, and he collapses onto her. She can hear Ethan's cries, as he is eased out of the van, and gloved arms reach in to lift Fretwell from on top of her. It seems like minutes before they are separated, but it can only be a few seconds.

As Fretwell's body is pulled away, she sees a bloody gash on the side of his face where his ear used to be. She spits it out, and wipes her mouth on her sleeve, suddenly disgusted.

Uniformed arms reach for her, and the pain in her leg suddenly takes over. Paramedics arrive, and as she lies on her back in this benighted van she now notices a dozen or more neat holes in the panelling above her.

Ethan is the first to be rescued, plucked from the van by an armed policeman and passed to green-uniformed paramedics who are emerging from an ambulance a few yards away.

Catherine only hears his heartfelt cries.

'Ethan!' she wails. 'I want Ethan.'

'He's just here,' she hears a woman say from a few yards away. 'He's fine. He is absolutely fine.' Two male paramedics gently ease Catherine onto a stretcher, the knife handle still protruding from her leg. They carry her across to the welcoming open doors of the ambulance, from which Ethan's sobs can be heard. A female paramedic has Ethan in her arms. 'Look,' she says. 'There's your brave mummy. What a courageous mum, eh? Now you just stay calm while we treat this leg for her.'

The paramedic places the child in Catherine's arms. 'Shhh, Ethan,' she says. 'Everything is going to be all right now.'

For me, time is standing still. The job is done, and I feel relief. A great light bathes me and I'm drawn up, through the van roof, through the car park and into a rufous night sky, high over Manchester. Higher and higher I go, lights above me dazzling, and then I hear voices, calling my name. They ask if I hear them, but I cannot speak to reply. I cannot open my eyes, I cannot move. I feel a touch on my face, and I smell the characteristic medicinal aroma which can mean only one thing. I am in a hospital. I was dead, but now, somehow, I am alive.

Editor's Note – Geoffrey Blake suffered grievous wounds in the attack, and his heart stopped beating on a dozen occasions. He was put into a medically induced coma, and ventilated artificially. However, doctors were unable to resuscitate him. Mr Blake remained unconscious, his organs only functioning through artificial support. It was Catherine Blake who after a week realised that the movement of her husband's eyelids was actually an attempt to communicate. He was suffering from locked-in syndrome, which meant he could hear her and see her, and by blinking, laboriously express himself. Over the next few weeks, with the help of a newly available brain–computer interface and a specialist team from London's Royal Marsden Hospital, he was able to dictate an account of his experience. He remained open-minded about his out-of-body journey, and whether or not he could see and hear everything that appeared in this account.

On midsummer's day, eight weeks after he was attacked, and shortly after finishing his account, Geoffrey Blake died. He was 43. His wife set up the Geoffrey Blake Trust to raise awareness of the problems of gang violence.

Death in the Van, *by Geoffrey and Catherine Blake, will be in published in October. This extract appears in this newspaper by kind permission of the publishers and the Geoffrey Blake Trust, to which a share of royalties from this book will be donated.*

Chapter Fifteen

Montpellier, France

Catherine

It is two years and one month since Geoff died, and I think about him every day. Ethan is a healthy three-year-old, and seems to have adapted well, though every so often he stops, looks around, and then turns to me to ask the two word question.

'Where Daddy?'

I tell Ethan that Daddy is up with the angels. 'But he'll be looking over you, darling, and watching out for you for ever and ever.' Perhaps this is a part of my rekindled Catholicism. I do still feel him, somehow.

We are renting a nice two-bedroom flat here, 15 minutes' walk from the sea. It is just after ten a.m. and I'm sitting at a pavement cafe, with Ethan in his pushchair. I've a croissant and a cup of coffee in front of me, and as I write, I feel the warmth of the sun on my legs. *Death in the Van* has been out for a year, and was briefly a *Sunday Times* bestseller. Inevitably, that meant I got more intrusive and personal attention from the media than I felt comfortable with, or was good for Ethan. So I made the difficult decision to leave Manchester. Coming here has been a welcome respite. No one knows me, and that suits me fine. Despite everything, I still have more of my story to tell, ready for when I will one day tell Ethan.

I wasn't there, of course, when Geoff was taken to Manchester Royal Infirmary, nine-tenths dead. I was being dragged to the damned Transit van, a gun to my head. But when the siege was over, almost twelve hours later, and I was being treated in hospital for my leg wound, he was foremost in my thoughts. I was told about his injuries, and the induced coma he had been put in while they bypassed his failing heart and supported his other vital functions. He had suffered nine stab wounds, and lost nearly two litres of blood. Some of this had leaked into his punctured lung, threatening to suffocate him. It was only the miraculous and indefatigable work of the paramedics that prevented him dying from shock and loss of blood, right there on the tarmac of Claremont Road.

When I was able to visit Geoff in intensive care, I was shocked by what I saw. He didn't look like the man that I knew and loved. He looked much older, but also serene, as if he accepted that he would never recover. Ethan, who was in my arms, called out to him, and with the nurses' permission I held our son close to his face. 'Kiss dadda, Ethan,' I said, trying to hold back my own tears. Ethan's kiss and tiny caressing hand on Geoff's cheek was one of the most moving things I have ever seen. He seemed to know that he had to be incredibly gentle. 'What a little angel,' said one of the nurses, who herself was in tears. Ethan wailed piteously when we had to leave, even as I explained that Daddy needed more care from the doctors before we could see him again.

Each day, I was wheeled in from an adjacent ward so I could spend a precious ten minutes with my husband. Doctors told me it was not any of the stab wounds, but a brain injury caused by Liam Fretwell's kick to the base of his skull that had caused the damage and prevented him from regaining consciousness. Over the course of that first week, before I understood that he could communicate, I held his hand and stroked his face, and told him that I loved him. Over those days, and perhaps as much for my own peace of mind as his, I gradually told him my story of captivity. I described how I had never stopped thinking about him, what a brave little man Ethan had been, and how the actions of the police had saved our lives. I filled him in on what the newspapers were saying. It was a huge comfort to me, even though Geoff eventually died never having regained what we call consciousness.

But today lack of consciousness has not quite the finality it once had. It was on the eighth day, I think, that I noticed the rhythmic twitching of his left eye. I had read years ago about locked-in syndrome and wondered if my husband could perhaps hear what I was saying. I asked him to stop blinking, and he did. Then I asked him to blink just once if he could hear what I said.

His eyelid lifted a tiny fraction, showing a sliver of moist eyeball, and then slid down again. There was an immediate spike in his heart rate.

From there things moved fast, as you will have read in the media. The coverage of Geoff's case was quite extensive. I remain profoundly grateful that he was able to communicate after such terrible injuries. That I could tell him how much I loved him, and that he could respond, and know that both Ethan and I had survived relatively unharmed. The incredible visions he had seen, the out-of-body experience, the flying he described, all amazed me. The whole thing had been so vivid, and he had accurately seen and experienced so much that I endured, just as if he was there with me. Those who say there is no God have to explain that. I certainly can't.

I barely edited Geoff's monologue, which is almost exactly as he gave it to me. I was astounded that he could express himself at all, so rather than quibble or correct some of his impressions, or what surely must have been imaginings, I let them stand. However, his vivid recollections of what happened to Ethan and me, his apparently detailed knowledge of the motivations and actions of the police and gang members, must have fed on what he overheard from me, and on what the police had let me know afterwards.

And this, I am afraid, is where the great unravelling begins.

I didn't tell Geoff everything. And just a little of what I told him was untrue. The lies, thanks to me, are woven in to his account. You won't spot them. It's quite seamless. It helps that there was no one to contradict my version of events. Fretwell and Cousins are dead, and Ethan is still a baby. Only I really know what happened in that van. And it is not, quite, the story that was told by Geoff.

So let's start again at the beginning, with what really happened on that hideous afternoon, and the first, startling untruth.

Geoff, poor thing, died convinced that what happened was a random collision of events. Two desperate criminals caught up with an innocent bystander and her child. That Ethan and I were simply in the wrong place at the wrong time. Pure bad luck.

It wasn't that way at all.

I had arranged to be there.

Oh, Geoff. I am broken hearted without him, and laden with guilt. He died believing the best of me, with no idea of what I was capable. He had no idea of the lies I have told, not just to him, but in my statement to the police. Some lies are omissions of truth, excised not only from my account of that day, but from our life. Some of these perhaps don't matter. Like the subterfuge over the deli. It's an easy one, so let me start with that.

There was a long shopping list for that store, because I had asked Geoff to cook us a Kurdish meal that evening. He was always delighted to prepare any meal I wanted, but Kurdish food was a new departure, and he had to research it on the Internet. But in truth I couldn't have cared less whether we had eaten Kurdish, Armenian or Moroccan that night. I just needed him to be in that particular shop for a good 15 minutes so that I could accomplish, without him noticing, a small and seemingly innocuous task. This turned out to be a disastrous errand carried out from a misplaced sense of guilt and pity, and from which almost all the subsequent deceits flow.

As I said, some of those falsehoods are unimportant. They don't matter. But some of them definitely do. You cannot understand my actions without knowing the original source of my sense of guilt. What from my Catholic childhood would be called my original sin.

Ethan wasn't my first child.

Yes, that's right.

I had been pregnant before. Years before. That time there was no IVF, no madcap copulation to an ovulation timetable. No praying for the miraculous, magical meeting of sperm and egg. And no gigantic expense. Not even a condom. None of that. The irony is that at 15 you conceive effortlessly. That's the age when you pray *not* to get pregnant. Another prayer not answered. I never told my devout parents, obviously, so it was easier not to tell Geoff either. My friend Megan, always there for me, helped me get a termination and persuaded me to go through with it when I wavered. The whole thing knocked me sideways. So when Geoff talked about me not doing well at school, he's right. But he doesn't know why. All he knows is that I failed several of my GCSEs, and that it took years for me to get back on track.

That deceit was never uncovered, and the guilt gnaws at me still.

But another omission of truth was discovered.

This one was a whopper.

It was late June, nine weeks after the abduction, and Geoff had been dead only a few days, having not quite got to the end of the story he wanted to tell. The funeral was to take place in three days' time. I was dreading it. But at least, once it was over, I thought all I would have to do was heal, learn how to sleep again, and to dedicate myself to bringing up my son. I was staying at my parents' house, doted on, enfolded in their love, and was also regularly visited by Geoff's mother and father, who had been incredibly supportive too. They did everything that loving families can.

How unworthy of all that love I now feel.

I tried to forget, I really did. But then something wriggled out from my nightmares and slid like a terminated and reproachful foetus, plop, into my waking life.

I was visited at home by the police. Detective Chief Inspector Ted Sampson, the senior officer in charge of the investigation, sat with his notebook open. He was a tall, fortyish man, quite well dressed in dark suit and tie, with steel-rimmed spectacles that intensified his gaze. Next to him was DC Emma Coughlan, maybe 35, in a grey trouser suit. They had always been friendly and kind when they took my statement all those weeks ago, and they were very polite and empathic this time too.

At first.

Sampson looked me in the eye and asked: 'We've been reviewing your statement, and there are just a few things that don't quite add up. I wonder whether you would be able to help us straighten them out.'

It was the kind of question I had been dreading, but as the weeks had worn on, I thought I might never have to face.

'It's really only a clarification,' DC Coughlan said, smiling at me. 'You are the only consistent witness across most of the events, so we rely on you to help connect the dots in the official account of this series of crimes.'

'According to your statement here,' Sampson said, 'You first saw Fretwell and Cousins in the rear-view mirror of your car. Then you heard them swearing, and turned to look.'

'Yes, that's right.'

'Then, after they had seized your vehicle, and the tragic stabbing of your husband, you were driven at speed through Moss Side.'

'Yes.'

'You mention a confrontation with the driver of another vehicle on the slip road into the Asda.'

'Yes.'

'We've traced the driver in question, and we've got a firm time for that event that corroborates what you told us.'

I nodded.

'And then you describe being left alone for a few moments while Fretwell and Cousins attacked Mr Singh and seized his van,' he said, flipping over the page of my statement. 'Then you witnessed the shooting of the two police officers.'

'Yes, that's right.'

'Mrs Blake. Were there any stops made in your car prior to its entry into the Asda, and before that confrontation?' Sampson's beady eyes were boring into my head.

'No. I mean I was really concentrating on Ethan and holding him close, but I would have noticed if we had stopped anywhere else.'

'Hmm. That's all entirely consistent as an account,' he said. 'But we have had an oddity emerge from the forensic tests.'

'Oh?' My heart was hammering.

'Yes,' Sampson said. 'As you will have read, Fretwell had that afternoon entered premises at 36 Badger Close and killed one Francis Douglas Sinclair.'

My stomach flipped over. 'Yes, I read about that. It was awful what they did to him.'

'They then went on to number 12 Walton Road, and killed Ms Lorraine Caldwell, whose body was found on the first floor landing.'

I nodded. I didn't trust myself to say anything at this point.

'Based on your account, we assumed both of those killings took place before your abduction,' Sampson said.

'The trouble, as we said, is that there is an anomaly,' Coughlan said. They looked at each other and then at me.

'We undertook DNA tests of the bloodstains in all locations,' Sampson said. 'In Mr Sinclair's home, in the common parts of the flats where Ms Caldwell died, in your car, in the stolen Transit van, and in the car park where the siege was concluded. It is routine procedure, even though in this case there is no one to prosecute.'

'It is the kind of thing that the coroner needs to know too,' Coughlan said, with a smile. 'Every family has the right to know the circumstances of their loved one's death.'

I nodded.

'Well the nub of it is this,' Sampson said. 'We discovered tiny traces of your husband's blood in Mr Sinclair's flat.'

I gave them my most confused look. 'How is that possible? He would never have been there.'

'No, no, sorry. We're not suggesting he was,' Sampson said. 'The blood was recovered from a footprint that matched the soles of Fretwell's footwear.' They both stared at me.

'I don't understand.'

'Neither do we,' Sampson said. 'If the events happened in the sequence we had assumed, then it would not be possible. Fretwell and Cousins have been very helpful, in some ways. They left a whole series of very messy crime scenes, walking in blood spillages, taking traces with them and depositing them at each successive scene. Forensically, this would tend to be cumulative, evidence from early crime scenes deposited at each later one. What is not easy to explain is how evidence from one of the later crime scenes came to be at what we had assumed was the first.'

I maintained my perplexed expression.

'Let me try and simplify this,' Coughlan said. 'We thought Mr Sinclair was killed *before* your husband was stabbed. But the forensic evidence would indicate that he was killed *later*.'

'Could the tests be wrong?' I asked.

Sampson shrugged. 'There is always the danger of contamination if evidence isn't correctly handled or labelled. But it's most uncommon, and we are extremely careful. It's awkward because the entire sequence of events, from what we assumed was the first death until the van's entry into the multi-storey car park is quite short, about ninety minutes. Time of death tests on the deceased aren't much help in sequencing deaths within such a narrow time frame, so we do rely on other forensics.' He leaned forward, elbows resting on his knees. 'Are you sure that there wasn't an additional stop on your journey around Moss Side? After the stabbing of your husband and before you were driven onto the Asda site?'

'I'm absolutely positive,' I said.

It was the most barefaced lie of my life. But I couldn't admit the truth. Because that would have changed everything.

It was a week later. Geoff had been buried, and I had been interviewed by the *Daily Telegraph*, the *Guardian*, and the *Manchester Evening News*. I had also been approached by publishers about turning Geoff's beyond-the-grave account into a book. There was, my newly acquired literary agent Camilla Tierney assured me, enough money for this type of true crime account to provide Ethan and me with modest financial security. She soon arranged for serialisation rights in the *Sunday Times*. I wasn't enthusiastic about being in the limelight, for reasons that will become clear, but felt so battered by events that I was happy to go with the flow.

Then the irritatingly thorough DCI Sampson began to unpick more of my fabrications.

I was asked to visit Longsight Police Station. Sampson and Coughlan weren't there at the appointed time, but turned up 15 minutes late, without apology. I took that as a bad omen. I was right to do so.

'We've rechecked the blood samples,' Coughlan said, without preamble, as we all sat down in a grey and unwelcoming interview room. 'The initial results were confirmed. It is your husband's blood on the tiles of Mr Sinclair's kitchen.'

Sampson took over. 'A neighbour upstairs from Mr Sinclair said she heard banging and shouting from the flat below, but didn't have any accurate record of the time. A bit before four, is the best she could tell us.'

I said nothing.

They then spent a half hour asking me all over again about the sequence of events in the abduction, and I stuck rigidly to my story. Finally, Sampson shrugged. 'Okay, Mrs Blake. Let's come at this from a different direction. We've been looking for Mr Sinclair's mobile phone. There was no sign of it in his flat, so we thought perhaps Fretwell or Cousins took it.'

'Have you found it now?' I hoped to God they hadn't. I'd watched Fretwell drop it down a drain. Something else that I hadn't mentioned in my statement.

Coughlan responded to my quizzical expression: 'No. We were hopeful that it might help us narrow down the time of death. So we contacted the Benefits Agency, which we knew would have a contact number for Mr Sinclair. Having got that, we were able to contact his service provider and get the metadata from the phone for that day, even though we don't possess the device.'

'What's the metadata?' I knew, but I was stalling for time.

'It's basically the list of numbers that he called, who called him, and when,' she said.

My entire body went cold and I felt a prickling of fear down my spine.

Sampson picked up the thread: 'And it seems the last call answered on that phone was 4.11 p.m. By that time we had assumed Mr Sinclair should already have been dead. According to all the timings we have, Fretwell and Cousins had just abducted you and your son at 4.06 p.m., and having stabbed your husband, were leaving Walton Road.'

'Mrs Blake, can you tell us who answered that last phone call on Mr Sinclair's phone and what they said?' Coughlan asked.

'I've no idea.'

'Really?' Sampson asked. 'You really should have. The last phone call received by Francis Sinclair before he was so brutally murdered was made from your own phone.'

Chapter Sixteen

I was stunned. Being caught out like this was the last thing I expected. As far as I knew, a phone in a sewer would take its secrets with it. I had to think fast, and I did.

'Fretwell demanded that I give him my phone,' I said. 'There was someone who owed him money, who I presume was Sinclair. By ringing him on my phone he wouldn't arouse any suspicions.'

The two police officers exchanged a glance. 'That's a nice try, Catherine,' said DCI Sampson. 'If that was the only call, I would buy your explanation. But in fact there was a blizzard of calls between you and Mr Sinclair in the fifteen minutes immediately before you were taken hostage. How do you explain that?'

I said nothing.

'Let me help you,' he continued. 'There are two possibilities, as I see it. Either you were taken hostage a good quarter of an hour earlier than you claimed, and Fretwell and Cousins were already using your phone. Or you have some kind of pre-existing connection to Francis Sinclair. Which is it?'

I said nothing.

Coughlan showed me a piece of paper. 'Mrs Blake, do you know what this is?'

I took a glance at the official-looking document. 'It says it's a warrant signed by a magistrate.'

'Yes, Catherine. We know Francis Sinclair left three voicemails on your phone between 3.43 p.m. and 4.05 p.m. on the day he was killed. This warrant allows us go to your phone service provider and force them to disclose to us the content of those messages. We want to hear what it was that he so desperately wanted to tell you.'

I said nothing.

'It would save us an awful lot of trouble if you just told us now,' Sampson said. 'We're really not anxious to bring charges against you for perverting the course of justice, but we certainly could if you don't co-operate.'

Coughlan gave me an icy smile. 'Catherine, you're a media heroine at the moment, but there's nothing the press enjoy more than dragging people down to size. And the fact you lied to the British public would be big news. I'd think about that if I was you.'

I put my head in my hands and cried for a few minutes. Then I finally decided to tell the truth. So here it is.

Chapter Seventeen

I ran into Francis Sinclair two years ago. I was running a drop-in open day, Learning for the Disabled, in a community hall in Moss Side. It was something I did about once a month since FuturePerfectSkills had been awarded the contract by the local authority. I was working from a cramped office, laptop balanced on a small desk, while Heather, an outreach worker from the Citizens Advice Bureau, took details in the main hall before the clients came in to see me. It had just gone noon, and the morning session was finished, when Heather knocked. 'Just one more appointment, Catherine. This is Mr Sinclair, he has had trouble getting here in time,' she said. What I saw was a unkempt and rather grubby middle-aged man in a wheelchair. The fact he was missing a leg was obvious from the end of one filthy trouser leg tucked underneath him. He was lean and gaunt, with a hawk-like expression, and long, greasy hair, carefully parted. A liberal dusting of dandruff sat on the broad shoulders of his worn jacket, and he emanated an unwashed aroma. A neatly knotted tie dangled over his once-white shirt, now grey with age.

Still, it was evidence that he had, in his own terms, made an effort.

She offered to help him wheel his chair through the narrow doorway, but he would have none of it. I was already halfway through greeting him when I recognised him. He had pale green eyes, set deep in his head, which gave his gaze an astonishing intensity.

The officialese description of him I would later type into the computer was of a disabled man, aged 45, with mental health issues, debt and housing problems, loneliness and an alcohol dependency.

But I knew him.

Sparko. Frankie 'Sparko' Sinclair. I had not seen him for 24 years. I recognised him, even though I was shocked by the deterioration in his circumstances and appearance.

He was the father of my first, terminated, baby.

And I had never told him.

The story isn't an untypical one. The Sinclairs were near neighbours of ours, having moved from Glasgow a couple of years before. I knew Sparko's younger sister Lisa, who I went to school with. We weren't close friends, particularly, but she invited me to her sixteenth birthday party one day in July. With the parents away, it was the usual teenage riot of loud music, drunkenness and heavy petting. That's where I first met Lance Corporal Sparko Sinclair, who was on leave. Lisa's parents had foolishly asked him to make sure the party didn't get out of hand. He was six years older, a Royal Engineer, and as handsome a man as any 15-year-old girl had ever seen. He was a bit of a George Best to look at back then, the dark hair, the piercing eyes and an irresistibly cheeky grin. My adult self might now like to persuade you that our one-night stand was a case of drunken, vulnerable me being taken advantage of by an older man of dubious motives, but let's face it, the time for lying is over. I am going to be honest. I knew exactly what I was doing. I wanted him, he wanted me.

We barricaded ourselves in Lisa's parents' bedroom, moving a bedside table against the door. It was my first time, but I enjoyed it, even while understanding that it would probably not be repeated. We both knew it. His unit was being posted to Cyprus in a week. It might as well have been the moon.

So meeting Sparko again, I was hungry to hear his story. Most people, learning he had served in the Gulf War and later in Iraq, jumped to conclusions about the loss of his leg. And no, it wasn't caused during his time in the British Army. It became quickly clear to me that damage had been done to him in those conflicts, particularly in Iraq, but it was more subtle and unseen. If he'd lost a limb then, he would now have a state-of-the-art prosthetic. Military veterans tend to get additional help in these things. But he'd actually lost the leg through an untreated infection after a heroin overdose in 2010. By that time he had also been in and out of prison, and was an alcoholic. To be fair to the NHS, the most significant obstacle to his being able to get a prosthetic was his terminal inability to keep a hospital appointment, look after himself, or stick to his medication. Many people might have said his bad luck was of his own making, and you can see their point.

Others, the kind of people I work with, people like me in fact, would excuse it all as a symptom of his post-traumatic stress disorder. Bad behaviour is always easier to excuse if there is a medical name for it. He's not bad, he's just 'alternatively moralled', as the old joke has it. So people like me tended, by default, to sympathise with people like Sparko. Until they heard about how he beat up his wife, now his ex-wife. If they had seen the pictures of what he actually did to her, then the sympathy tended to evaporate.

But I only knew all that much later. Sparko did a fabulous job of keeping me in the dark, just as I had done to him in the past.

'So, Mr Sinclair, what kind of skills are you looking to acquire?' It was my standard introduction, but it ended in an awkward cough, and I took a moment to recover. He didn't seem to recognise me.

'I've already got what skills I need. But no one needs one-legged electricians,' he said. 'I was wondering if you could help with these.' He had brought with him a carrier bag stuffed with unpaid and, in many cases, unopened bills. He had various benefit forms too, including the notorious 90-page appeal form to try to reinstate his Disability Living Allowance. That alone I knew would take at least two hours to fill in. He also needed an appeal letter written so that he didn't lose his adapted Motability car, on which he had fallen behind with the payments. The final issue he mentioned was that he was two months behind on the rent, and had been threatened with eviction.

I did what I could. I made appointments with the CAB debt, housing and benefit specialists, and typed him up a holding letter for his car, though I warned him that it was unlikely to stop him losing the vehicle.

'Och, that's all right, lassie. I sold it two months ago.'

'You sold it?'

'Aye. I needed the cash.'

'You can't do that! It wasn't yours to sell.'

He smiled, a knowing grin of those who live life in a different world. 'Aye, but if you were in my shoe,' he paused to let the word take effect, 'you'd have done the same. I just don't want to go to court again when they come for it and cannae find it.' He began to roll a cigarette, and I had to remind him that he couldn't light up in the community centre. He stowed the fag behind his ear. I flicked through the Motability paperwork and then, on the original 2010 application, found my husband's signature as a referee. Until that moment I hadn't known that Geoff had once been his probation officer. When I told Sparko, he expressed surprise that Geoff was my husband. He was even more surprised that Geoff had given up his probation career within a year of that application.

It became clear that Sparko faced the kind of day-to-day problems that few of us can imagine. He had slept rough in the past, and had few possessions, so wasn't that bothered about the prospect of losing the flat. He just wanted enough money coming in to charge his phone, have a pint or two and keep him in rolling tobacco. I had to remind him that without an address or a functional bank account, getting any kind of benefits was going to be difficult. I finished by encouraging him to come again, and see Heather, who would work through his problems with him.

'I'd rather see you, lassie,' he responded. He fixed me with a knowing thin-lipped smile. 'Cathy, isn't it? Been a long time, eh.'

Chapter Eighteen

I went home that evening in a state of shock. It was the amazement that two lives can cross so briefly, and diverge so fundamentally before crossing again. I was buried under a lorry-load of guilt: for my own good fortune, which I was convinced I didn't deserve, for having an abortion, for not consulting the father-to-be in advance and for not telling him afterwards. Most of all, I felt ashamed for keeping all of it from Geoff. Meeting Sparko had churned it all up.

It was several months before I saw Sparko again. When I finally saw his name on the appointment list my heart gave a little bump. The chance to make amends. I know, pathetic isn't it? But there you are, that's what guilt does. He was late, and I stayed an extra 40 minutes, missing my own lunch break, in case he showed up.

He finally did.

He looked better too. A new jacket, better trousers, a bit more of the old twinkle in those dazzling eyes. He didn't smell quite as ripe as he had before, either. Our meeting was quite businesslike. I checked through the casework, and found that he'd had some improvement. A specialist CAB housing caseworker had successfully petitioned the court for a delay in eviction proceedings pending the decision on his benefit appeal. That might take several more weeks, but in the meantime she had got him housing benefit and council tax benefit too.

'Things are looking up, Sparko,' I said. 'You just need to get on top of these debts.'

'Aye, true enough. But I'm still skint.'

Just then I looked up at him. 'How much actual cash have you got to live on?'

'Now?' He rummaged in his pockets and laughed. 'I've got forty pence to my name.'

'When did you last eat?'

'Yesterday evening. I go to the kebab house at closing, and they let me have scraps.'

'That's not very good for you.'

'Aye, but it's better than nothing.' Perhaps it was shame, but he changed the subject and asked me about myself. Whether I had children, whether I was married. I gave him a summarised version. I said that Geoff and I had wanted to have kids, but didn't mention that we were still trying with IVF. The disappointments, the sickness from the drugs, the miscarriages, and of course the cost. That bundle of pain and longing, that would have been a disclosure too far.

'I'd like to have been a father,' he said, shaking his head. 'But it's no gonna happen now. I'm a fucking mess, and no mistake. I've had money, and I've run through it. So I'm broke again.'

I felt a new wave of shame and guilt. Part of me was desperate to confess to the abortion, to ask for absolution. Anything to dull the keen knife of guilt.

Sparko was surprised I had married his old probation officer, but approved of the match. 'One thing, lassie. Dinnae mention to your husband that I'm still struggling. He had high hopes for me getting work when I came out of clink.'

'No, I won't. As I said, he's not a probation officer anymore, and I'm bound by rules of confidentiality in any case.'

I opened my handbag as I was about to leave. He put his hand firmly on my arm and said: 'Don't give me money, lassie. I couldnae bear it.'

'I was just looking for my car keys.' In truth I had considered offering him £20. Things were tight enough at home, but I felt a responsibility for him. His rejoinder had reminded me that he still had something of his dignity left to save. He had the outreach centre phone number already, but I also gave him my mobile number. 'Just in case of emergency,' I explained.

That was unprofessional. Though I wasn't a social worker, I'd undergone very similar training. As had Geoff, of course. All the instruction stipulates the same thing. Don't get involved. Don't let your natural sympathy overcome your professional detachment. Easier said than done of course. The whole reason anyone wants to work with the homeless, the poverty-stricken or the disabled is out of a natural sympathy, and of course the middle-class guilt so many of us are marinated in. The truth is that professional detachment is easier to aspire to than to achieve. I, of course, failed miserably.

But at first, it was okay. He didn't ring, and I forgot about it.

My God, I had no idea what I'd let myself in for.

Chapter Nineteen

It was a couple of months later when I next saw him, by appointment, to review the debts and benefit situation. He was late again. I was waiting for him in the drop-in centre, watching the ramp in case he needed a push. 'Hello Cathy,' he said.

I turned around, and he was there, standing just a few feet away. He'd come up the steps to the side entrance. On two feet. He was genuinely well turned out, in another smart jacket, new white shirt and shoes so well polished you could see your face in them. I suppose some things about the army never leave you. His hair was trimmed and tidy too.

'I've got me new leg fitted, finally,' he explained, pointing to the prosthesis.

'What did happen to the original one? You never told me.'

'A couple of head cases took it, as insurance.'

'Insurance for what?'

'Never mind. But the NHS were not best pleased. It's taken me a long time to regain their trust. And I need to keep to my physio appointments. They are saying that I can't take the bus until the leg's settled in, like. And I cannae afford a taxi.'

'I might be able to give you a lift if you can fix the appointment times to suit.'

So that is what happened. I was really impressed with how he had turned his life around, and over the next few months we got into a routine that fitted around my Tuesday lunchtime, while his physio appointments lasted. But that's to get ahead of myself. As I was leaving, he said: 'You seem very fidgety today, lassie.'

'Do I?' Not for the first time, I realised, Sparko was spookily perceptive. I was due to have an IVF appointment later that afternoon, and was hopeful for some good news. It was certainly costing enough, and I had used up my free NHS attempts. A few days ago I had had a fertilised egg transferred back into my womb, and it was time to see if it had implanted successfully.

'It's okay,' he said, almost as if he had a direct line into my head. 'It's going to be good news, I promise ye.'

'I hope so.'

'You'll make a terrific mother.'

And it was good news. The fertilised egg, the microscopic bundle of cells that was destined to be Ethan, had implanted successfully. It was almost as if Sparko had willed it. If so perhaps it was a reward for helping him. My atonement.

I didn't tell the police all of this. I described to them the work I was doing with him, helping him put his life in order. In theory

I shouldn't have, because much of Sparko's circumstances were covered by client confidentiality. But now he was dead it didn't seem to matter. He was never one for bureaucratic niceties even when he was alive. If he had been able to fill out forms unaided then he would never have been in the dire straits that he was. Besides, I had my own skin to save by co-operating with the police.

Everything I'd told them up to this point was reasonable. My connection with Sparko Sinclair was a legitimate part of my work, for all that I had failed to keep a professional distance. But there's no crime in that. The police knew it too. What they really wanted to hear about was the last time that I met Sparko. They had a hunch it was important. They were right.

Chapter Twenty

It was the day before the abduction. He had rung me up and asked to meet in a cafe in Levenshulme, a different part of Manchester, a couple of miles from his usual stamping ground. 'I can't go to the drop-in centre anymore,' he said.

It was out of my way, but I went during my lunch break. He was half an hour late. I was disappointed, because the last three or four times when I had given him lifts to his physio appointments he had been punctual. But when I saw him, my intentions to berate him for his failings went out of the window. He was back in the wheelchair and looked smaller somehow, anxious and fidgety. He had not looked after his appearance. There were drifts of dandruff on his jacket and there was a red, scurfy rash visible on his scalp.

I bought him a coffee, and found us a secluded table. 'You look terrible, Sparko.'

'Aye,' he said, staring out of the window, scanning the street. 'Things have been a wee bit tough recently.'

'What happened to your new leg, then?'

He looked down as if he hadn't realised that last time he been able to walk around. 'Oh, that. It's got a wee bit uncomfortable. Life's been a bit complicated. I've had to move flats in a hurry, like.' He scratched at his stump and winced.

'It looks painful.'

He shrugged, and his gaze again returned to the window. A black BMW cruised past slowly, and Sparko shrank down into his chair below window height until it had gone. 'Aye, it's sore and weeping like a bairn.'

'What does the hospital say?'

'I haven't been. I daren't.'

'Why on earth not?' I was a little angry with him for the backsliding. But I hadn't a clue.

'Have you ever experienced fear, lassie? I mean the kind of terror that turns your bowels to water and stops you sleeping at night?'

'Not really.' I could have mentioned the skin cancer, but I didn't want to divert him from what he wanted to say. I expected some revelation about his time in Iraq perhaps some insight into how his life had fallen to pieces. I wanted to give him the space to expand on this. That's how hungry I was for his story. But I was completely wrong.

'I've got enemies. Powerful, dangerous, ruthless people. Right here in Manchester.'

'Do you mean those head cases you mentioned?'

'Aye, it's the guy they answer to. Liam Fretwell. Seven years ago he asked me to look after something for him. Until he got out.'

'He's in prison?'

'He was, aye. Wakefield. And he should have been for many more years. But I heard yesterday he's on the loose and the whole gang is looking for me. I got out just in time.'

'Have you been to the police?'

The look he gave me was one of incredulity, as if I was suggesting he escape by building a spaceship to fly to another planet.

'Fer fuck's sake, lassie.' He shook his head at my stupidity. 'They've got eyes and ears in the peelers. I can't go back to my old flat, I can't risk seeing my old cronies, and I wouldn't trust them anyway. They'd track me down even at the drop-in centre or the hospital. I'm not exactly hard to follow.'

'Was it money?'

He eyed me carefully before replying, as if deciding whether to trust me or not. 'Aye. Mostly cash. For years I was good at taking care of it, but when things got tight I dipped in. I thought, I'll just spend a wee bit. Then when I got into debt I spent a bit more. I thought, it's nae problem. I know horses, I know form. I can win it back. And maybe Fretty'll never come back. But then I lost more. And now there's none of the readies left.'

'How much?'

'Fifty grand, give or take.'

My indignant voice climbed at least an octave: 'Fifty thousand? You've been through fifty thousand pounds and have nothing to show for it?' I thought of how he could easily have paid off his debts, sorted his housing problems, even paid for a better prosthesis and a physio to visit him.

He laughed. 'Aye. It's the old joke. I spent most of it on whores, booze and the gee-gees. And the rest I wasted. All that's left now from the holdall that he gave me to look after is the difficult stuff. When a pair of legs would be handy. And a car.'

'Why did he give it to you?'

'That's a fine question.' Sparko took a deep breath. 'Back in those days Fretty lived upstairs from me down in Moss Side. He was a tearaway even as a teenager, and I knew he was a gangster. Occasionally I'd have a drink with him, but he was like nitroglycerin. Ready to blow at any time. Eventually, I learned to stay away.'

He stared into his coffee cup. 'There was one summer night. Five in the morning, the police raided his flat. Ten of 'em at least, come roaring up the stairs, battered his door down. Terrible racket they made, on my ceiling. I learned later that Fretty had just the day before killed two members of a rival gang and stolen their cash and gear. I'm a heavy sleeper, but was woken by the noise, and then by the hammering of the bobbies on my door. They seemed to be waking everyone in the block. So I got up, hauled myself onto the chair, and wheeled myself to my front door. Some WPC asked me if I'd seen him and I told her the truth. I hadn't. They came into the sitting room, stayed a few minutes, which is all the time anyone wants to be in my pigsty, then let me go back to bed. But as soon as I got myself into the kitchen for a brew, I saw Fretwell, in trackie bottoms, no shirt or shoes, squeezing out from the larder. He had a fucking gun and was pointing it at me.'

'Good grief.'

'Aye. When he heard the peelers roaring up the stairs, he'd jumped out of his bathroom window upstairs, landed in the grass at the back, and climbed in through mine, which was an achievement as it was only open a wee notch. He was scared. It was the only time I'd ever seen him scared. Nineteen years old, already a double murderer and facing life inside. He warned me to keep quiet, and pulled out this big, ripped holdall from under my sink. He cursed me because he'd broke the bag handles trying to get in through my window. As if it was my fault.'

'What did you do?'

'Aye, well it was tricky. They'd posted a plod on the entrance to the flats, probably until the crime scene laddies came in the morning. The back way was all right, but you cannae get a car in because of the bollards. Fretwell knew he couldn't run out in bare feet, lugging this knackered blue bag and expect to get away. And I'm the guy who can only lend him one shoe. He made a couple of calls, and slammed the phone on the counter top in disgust. The police were raiding everywhere, and none of his mates could come out for him. So he stuffed the holdall back in the larder, and said to me, and I remember every word: "You are going to look after this for me, all right? Should be tonight I get back, but who knows. I know exactly what's there, I've counted it. If anything is missing when I get back, I'll fucking kill you, right? I'll fucking *kill* you. You can't run from me. If I go down, I've got friends on the outside who will find you. Breathe a word and you're dead. If I don't get back tonight, put it somewhere safe. Then let me know. Behave yourself and I'll see you all right".'

'That's pretty scary,' I said.

'Aye. The peelers got him six hours later after a chase on the M60.'

'So what else was in the bag?'

Again he hesitated before replying. 'Wads of foreign currency. I had a go at getting some changed at a travel agent place a few months ago, but they started asking lots of questions and I lost my bottle, to be honest. Then there were drugs, tablets mainly. I've no idea what they were, or what they were worth. It's all stuff that's hard to dispose of unless you have the contacts. And it would be a giveaway. How many one-legged men deal drugs in the city?'

'I see your point.'

'Fretwell's first message to me arrived within two days of his arrest. Two black guys, one of them enormous, came for me. When I opened the door they just picked me up and tossed me on the settee. "Fretwell's got a message for you," they said. They slapped me about a bit, and then took my NHS leg. "Just in case you had ideas of running away," the big guy said. They almost pissed themselves laughing at that.'

'That's terrible,' I said.

'Aye, but I don't think they had a clue I was actually looking after so much gear. I reckon they thought it I just owed Fretwell a grand or two from some loan sharking. I mean, who would trust a broken-down alky like me with so much cash, and the other stuff. Jesus. Otherwise they might have tried to get it for themselves.'

'So what did you do?'

'I had already hidden the cash inside my TV. It was one of those old, heavy jobs, last of the cathode ray tubes. It's deep, and there's a lot of space inside. I got a new sports bag for all the other gear, and took it in a taxi to the lock-up garage I had rented for my old Motability car, until I came up with a better idea.'

I looked at him quizzically.

'Lassie, I'm not going to tell ye the details. It's nae your business. There's nothing you can do to help. I'll be dead in a week and then you can get on with yer life and forget about old Sparko.'

'Don't talk like that.'

He gave a grim laugh. 'Did you read what Fretwell did to the guys at RHC22?'

'What's RHC22?'

'A rival gang. It stands for Right Hard C-words, pardon my French. There were twenty-two of them originally. There's not even twenty now, even if you add up the body parts.'

I shuddered. 'But there must be something you can do,' I said. 'So you've still got this stuff?'

'I know where it is. But I was stupid. One of the Moss Side Mafia guys came to visit a week ago, to remind me that Fretwell was coming for his money. It sounded like a hint that the prison break was coming. So I had this fucking genius idea to hide the loot better. Now I cannae get at it for the moment, and it's my own fault for trying to be too clever.' He sighed and drained the remains of his coffee. 'Jesus, even if I could get it, I couldnae spend it easily.'

I gave a deep sigh, finished up my coffee and checked the time. 'That's quite a tale, but I've got to go.' I took his hand. 'You've got to look after yourself, Sparko. Stay away from these people. Forget the money. Leave Manchester.'

He looked up at me. 'I've got nae money to dae it. Besides, they'd find me eventually.' He paused. 'Ten years ago I would be able to look after myself, maybe even with Fretwell. But now, with this,' he gestured at his leg. 'I'm helpless.'

'Well, not completely. There's the CAB, there's Heather, and me.'

He looked out of the window. 'You're a good person, Catherine. There's no one else in my life that I can trust.' It wasn't intended as a question. I muttered something self-deprecatory. Then I said something stupid, something that laid me and my son open to everything that subsequently happened. It was something that anyone might say. But after saying it, putting out the open invitation, the slippery slope I was already on with Sparko just got a whole lot greasier. I later realised that it was exactly what he had been angling for, since the start of the conversation.

I said: 'Sparko, I can't bear to think of you in danger. Isn't there anything I can do, anything at all?'

He was clever, was Sparko. He didn't immediately blurt it out, but played me a little more line, a little bit more bait, which I gulped down. 'I cannae ask you, lassie. These are my problems and I should deal with them myself.' He stared off into the middle distance, sucking his teeth. I suddenly thought that he was going to ask me if he could stay at our place, and that would simply be impossible. Please don't ask me that, I thought.

It was a non-starter. I couldn't begin to explain to Geoff. I was middle class enough to realise that while I didn't mind dealing with a smelly and untrustworthy ex-prisoner in my work, I was never going to invite one into my home. Who would?

It was, again, as if he had read my mind. 'It wouldnae be right for me to ask to stay at your place, you with a bairn and all,' he said. He then paused for a second, and switched on his old charm. 'Look, there is a tiny wee thing that would really help. I can't risk being seen at my old flat now, but there should a new shock-absorbing pad for my leg coming for me in the post tomorrow. Could you pick it up for me?'

'That shouldn't be any problem,' I replied. 'It's definitely coming tomorrow then?'

'Well, it's eBay, and I've been waiting for it to come from Germany for a month, but Wednesday delivery is what they told me. It would also be good to go when the nosy bitch upstairs isn't there. Lorraine's always out from three until four in the afternoon on a Wednesday at her ex's mam, so the poor bampot who was once married to her can have visiting rights for the bairn.'

'She's not someone you like, then?'

'You could say that, aye.' He looked at me. 'It's not her, it's who she knows. Who she might tip off. But I shouldnae worry. You won't be in any danger. You don't look like one of my friends, she wouldnae twig, like.'

'So what *do* I look like?' I was genuinely curious.

'I'd say a social worker, a housing officer, summat like that. An educated woman, obviously. But still best not to run into

Lorraine Caldwell. And if you go exactly when I've asked, you willnae. It's as simple as that.'

He handed me a bunch of keys, and identified the largest, which was for the communal front door in the three-floor walk-up. 'Could you just ring me the moment you get there, lassie? This leg is so uncomfortable at the moment, and is giving me blisters, which is why I cannae wear it. These German pads are supposed to be a wonder. I need to know straightaway, like.'

'Of course,' I responded. It wasn't much to ask, was it?

I knew the address. Walton Road. It was one of tens of thousands of 1960s low-rise flats around that part of Manchester. It was on a side road just a few doors away from our favourite deli. So although it might take a bit of organising, I thought I could fit this two-minute errand into the rest of Wednesday's chores without any significant disruption. Easy, really. In fact I was so relieved that Sparko hadn't asked anything difficult of me, that I was more than happy to rearrange my day, our day, around it. Just picking up post! Phew. Favours like that are easy to grant.

If only I had known.

I would have refused on the spot.

Chapter Twenty-One

Sparko Sinclair had me on a string, it has to be said. DCI Sampson smirked when I told him that the task turned out to be nothing to do with the post. He wasn't surprised at all. The police knew all about Sparko's lies and evasions over many years. He wasn't expecting a parcel at all. Fetching the post was simply a lure. He wanted to get me into the building at the required time, and use my phone call to him to switch the errand to something far more important. Bait and switch. The new task didn't seem a difficult errand either, but it was odd. Something that if he had told me about at the time, would have raised some suspicion.

Sampson and Coughlan nodded in agreement. 'So that whole expedition for groceries, buying Kurdish food at that particular store, was devised purely to be there at the right time, for Mr Sinclair?' Sampson asked.

'Well, we did use that store a lot, but the timing, basically, yes.'

'Why didn't you leave the child at home?' Coughlan asked.

'I had planned to. I had booked a babysitter, but she had rung me up early in the afternoon to cancel. I was annoyed, but it didn't seem that troublesome to have Ethan with us. Picking up post isn't supposed to be dangerous is it, even in Moss Side?'

I continued with my story of that Wednesday. After Geoff had parked the car outside the deli, and went in with a huge list of ingredients and delicacies he wanted to buy, I told him I was popping into the newsagents next door. I didn't of course. We were running late, but it wasn't yet quite ten to four. I still had a few minutes. I had kept the phone off all afternoon until then. It was only partly because of the hospital, although that was a decent excuse.

'Why was it then?' Coughlan asked.

I told her. I did it because I half expected a nervous Sparko to start ringing me, and I didn't want to have to explain those calls to Geoff. But the moment he went into the deli, I left Ethan in the car seat, and promised him I'd be back in two minutes.

'So you left your child alone in the car while you went in?' Coughlan asked.

'Yes, just for a minute or two. But I locked it and took the keys.'

'So what happened then?' Sampson asked.

Chapter Twenty-Two

Recalling it now, I am surprised I wasn't more scared. The front door to the building had opened easily. There was the smell of rubbish, stale cooking and something else unpleasant that I didn't want to think about. Sparko's flat was number two, and I had a key for it, though I wouldn't have needed it. The door had obviously been kicked in recently, and the lower panel was still broken. There was no one around, but I was still glad Sparko hadn't asked me to go into his home.

Looking down, there was indeed a sizeable pile of post on the floor. It would take minutes to go through. Something inside me was anxious to be quick. I felt I should just scoop it all up, and go through it somewhere else. Anything that wasn't Sparko's I could drop back through the door later, even another day. But there was no parcel. So I turned the phone on, and it rang immediately.

Before I could even speak, he was on to me, almost rude: 'What's been keeping yer?'

'I'm sorry. I told you I had other errands. The post…'

'Forget the fucking post. There's something else I forgot. Go upstairs to the top floor...'

'But your flat is on the ground floor.'

'Aye, that's right. That's why it's clever. Now shut up and listen, I don't have time to say this twice. On the left-hand wall of the top-floor corridor is the fuse box for the house.'

'Okay, hang on.' I ran up the stairs two at a time, my footsteps clattering. I reached the top floor, breathlessly, and felt for the light switch. A strip light flashed, buzzed then flickered on. The windowless corridor led to two front doors, painted municipal green. The first cupboard I found on the left was a wooden one. I described it to him. 'No, that's just the stopcock to the hot water tank. It's painted grey, come on lassie. Quick. It's only a couple of feet on.'

Then I spotted it. I had somehow expected it to be at waist height, but it was 18 inches high and 12 wide, built into the skirting board close to the nearest flat's front door. I crouched down, and fumbled for the small key on the ring that he said would fit it. Inevitably it was the last one I tried. Inside was an ancient rat's nest of electrics, brown fag packet-sized fuses, looping cables in different gauges and colours, and a large and more recent label with the local authority's logo warning about the danger of electrocution.

I heard a key in the outside door downstairs. The irritable voices of a woman and a young child carried up to me, then a slam. I crept back and peered down into the stairwell. The woman was berating the child for something and, having parked a pushchair, began to climb the stairs to the first floor, with the youngster in her arms. I returned to my task.

'She's back,' I whispered.

'Then hurry the fuck up,' Sparko said.

'It's all electrics. I might get a shock.'

'Not if you listen to what I say,' he retorted angrily. 'I'm a British Army-trained electrician. Flick the big Bakelite switch on the right up, that will cut the power.' I didn't know what Bakelite was, but I flipped the biggest switch. The building was plunged into darkness.

'Oi. What are you doing up there?' called the woman. Her voice was coarse and antagonistic.

I ignored her, to listen to Sparko, who said: 'Reach behind the circuit board. There's a key taped to it. That's the key I need.'

'It's dark,' I hissed, flicking the phone's light on. 'Now hang on while I put you on speaker.' As I hunted for the button, I heard the woman downstairs talking to someone. Not the child, the tone wasn't right. She too was on the phone.

'Okay, Sparko,' I said, holding the phone into the fuse box. 'I can see better now.'

'Don't use my fucking name, you moronic cow,' he bellowed, a voice that carried into the corridor. 'Now stick your hand down the back of the board on which the fuses are mounted.'

Furious with him, I did so. I couldn't find anything.

'It's not there,' I said.

'It must be. Feel further in.' But there was nothing. Sparko swore at me like I've never been sworn at in my life. It made me very angry.

Chapter Twenty-Three

I looked across the interview room table at the two detectives. 'There was nothing there.'

'So let me understand this correctly,' Sampson said. 'Mr Sinclair was trying to get you to retrieve a key from the fuse box of the flats.'

'Yes.'

'Did he ever tell you what this key was for?' Coughlan asked.

'No. It must've been something to do with the holdall of money and drugs, I suppose.'

'Oh, come on. Do you really think it was likely,' she continued. 'That Mr Sinclair, who as we know had only one leg, would have chosen to store a valuable key not only in the common parts of the building to which anyone had access, but would have chosen the second floor in a building with no lift, which would have made him the only resident unable to reach it.'

'If you think about it though, it's very clever isn't it?' I continued. 'It would be the last place anyone would look. For a start-off, Sparko was aware that his own flat was insecure. He wouldn't have been surprised that Fretwell would have started looking there. If Sparko had left the building his movements would not be hard to track. But if he chose the right time of day, he would be able given enough time to shuffle up the stairs on his bottom to place the key.'

'Why didn't he just take the key with him when he went to the new flat?' Sampson asked.

'I asked him that. He said he left in a frantic hurry on Sunday evening the moment he heard Fretwell was out, but Lorraine, the woman upstairs, was sitting smoking on the landing. He had complained to me before that she was often there for hours, playing with her phone, watching the kid shrieking as she rode in circles on her tricycle. He thought she was nosy.'

The two detectives looked profoundly sceptical. 'But in any case, the key wasn't there?' Sampson asked, his arms folded across his broad chest in scepticism.

'No, it wasn't.'

'So after he swore at you, what happened next?' he asked.

'I swore back at him and hung up.'

Chapter Twenty-Four

I was furious with Sparko for hoodwinking me into doing his dirty work. I flicked the Bakelite switch back on, and started to descend the stairs. The woman was standing at the bottom of the flight, looking up at me. 'Tell Sparko they're on their way for him,' she smirked. 'And for you.' I moved past her and walked down the next flight of stairs. Just as I was pushing open the outer door, she called to me from the landing. 'Is this what you are looking for?' she asked, dangling a small padlock-style key over the banister. I wasn't going to get involved in trying to grab it from her. If this key was what I thought it was, then it would bring nothing but trouble to Sparko. Better to let the gangsters have it. It was a one-minute walk back to the car, but seemed to take an hour. Halfway through it, I saw two rough-looking characters heading for the doorway that I had just exited. It was my first glimpse of Fretwell and Cousins.

I reached the car. I had been gone just five minutes, but Ethan was looking around anxiously and started to cry when he saw me. I knelt in the back and hugged him. I turned the phone on, wondering where Geoff was. 'Come on Geoff,' I said out loud, hoping that he would be nearly done. I dug out the car keys, but after resettling Ethan had barely time to think about moving the car, when I looked in the rear-view mirror. I saw them both then, running for our car. Fretwell and Cousins. Then the nightmare began in earnest.

Chapter Twenty-Five

Coughlan had been writing notes based on what I'd said. 'So when Sinclair rang, you didn't think it necessary to warn him that Fretwell and Cousins were coming for him?'

'That was only what the woman said—'.

'Lorraine Caldwell,' Sampson interjected.

'Yes. But I didn't know it for a fact. Also, I didn't know at the time that the two men I saw going into the building *were* Fretwell and Cousins. And I thought that Sinclair was safely in a new flat somewhere. I suppose with hindsight I should have warned him.'

Sampson looked up at me and then asked: 'So what really happened when Fretwell and Cousins got in your car?'

'They took my car keys off me, but didn't drive off straightaway. They demanded to know where Sparko was. I told them I didn't know, and Cousins immediately pointed the gun at Ethan and told me to ring him. Fretwell held up the key he'd got from Lorraine Caldwell, and showed it to me. "Ring him up and tell him you've got this," he said. "And you can bring it to him." So I did.'

Coughlan looked puzzled. 'But in an earlier call you'd already told Sinclair you couldn't find the key.'

'That's right, but I found a bit of inspiration. When Sparko answered I told him that I found the key in the base of the fuse box. I told him the tape had come off.'

'You are really quite creative aren't you?' Coughlan said, with a twisted smile on her face. I realised then that she didn't like me at all.

'I am telling you the truth,' I enunciated, my fists balled on the table.

'Well, you are now, finally,' Sampson said, with a sigh. 'So what was his reaction?'

'He was overjoyed. I said I was running behind, and I really wanted to just deliver the key to him so I could carry on with the rest of my day.'

'Did he give you his address?'

I didn't say anything for a while. 'He did, yes,' I whispered, finally. I looked down at the table, unable to meet their gaze.

'He trusted you, didn't he?' Sampson said.

'Yes. He said I was the only one he could trust.'

The two detectives looked at each other. Coughlan said: 'So Mrs Blake, you signed Sparko Sinclair's death warrant.' It wasn't a question. And my answer, my only possible answer, was simple:

'They were going to shoot Ethan. What could I do?'

Sampson was flicking back through his print-out of Geoff's book manuscript. 'Your husband's account, like your statement, describes him racing out of the shop the moment he saw

Cousins getting into the car. You wouldn't have had time to make the call to Sinclair, would you?'

'No, it was a good few minutes before Geoff noticed them in the car. It was one of the edits I had to make.'

They both stared at me. And this wasn't even halfway through the lies.

Chapter Twenty-Six

Sparko's new flat was two miles away, in a quiet cul-de-sac not far from the Asda. Fretwell may have driven like a maniac away from the shop, but for the sake of surprise he slowed right down when he went into Badger Close. They were 1980s red brick, already tatty, plastic bin sheds and ranch-style fencing around tiny weed-strewn patches of garden. There were cars parked all over the pavement. Number 36 stood out with its disabled ramp and handrail. 'Back in a mo,' Fretwell said, for all the world as if he was just going to buy a packet of fags.

What went on inside that flat I would never know but for the details carried in the press. Poor Sparko was bound and gagged with gaffer tape. Given that Fretwell was back in five minutes, I'd like to think that poor Sparko didn't suffer too much. But I think I know otherwise. The extra bloodstains on Fretwell's shirt as he walked back to the car told a story, though less eloquently than the broad grin on his face.

'It's the key for a lock-up garage,' Fretwell told Cousins. 'Got the address, with a bit of persuading.'

So that was where we headed off. The confrontation with the builder, the route around the back of the supermarket, the seizing of the Transit van, the shooting of the female officers: all that is true. The later in the siege we were, the more independent corroboration there was, and the more accurate Geoff's published account and my own original statement were. There was no need to change anything.

Chapter Twenty-Seven

Fretwell and Cousins were quite prepared to kill me and Ethan. They had said as much. My usefulness to them began as a tool for winkling out Sparko's new address. And then later, when they would happily have killed me because of what I knew, they kept me alive as a hostage. All that is true. However, I omitted from my statement to the police, even the revised one, some things that happened.

The police got closest to it when they asked again a week later to go over the details of the very start of the abduction.

'When did you first notice,' DCI Sampson asked. 'Bloodstains on Fretwell's clothing?'

'After he stabbed Geoff. He was covered in my husband's blood.' My tears began. 'I was screaming. It was awful.'

'I'm sorry, I didn't mean to upset you,' he said. 'It's just that as you know, they killed Lorraine Caldwell just before you were abducted. You were, as far as we can be aware, the last person to see her alive.'

'Well, we hardly exchanged a word,' I replied. 'She just gave me the warning and taunted me with the key.'

The two detectives looked at me, not speaking for quite a while. 'You say that she remained on the first floor while you were on the second, rummaging around in the fuse box.'

'That's right.'

'We found her fingerprints, along with yours, on the banister near the top of the stairs to the second floor. Can you think how that might have happened?'

'I suppose she went up there and discovered the key sometime earlier. Maybe that is why they killed her. For interfering. Maybe for taking the key for herself.'

'Plausible I suppose,' Sampson said, looking at Coughlan. 'It's as good a motive as we can think of. Fretwell never needed much excuse to kill someone.'

I'd been incubating a question for a while, hoping for a chance to pose it, innocently. 'So this sports bag of Fretwell's loot, did you recover it?'

Sampson blew an exasperated sigh. 'Not so far. Enquiries are ongoing. It wasn't in Mr Sinclair's own lock-up garage, so perhaps he had another we don't know about. But we know what should have been in it, because we know what RHC22 were robbed of all those years ago. Apart from the £57,300 in cash, and around 25,000 amphetamine tablets, we believe there was a lot of foreign currency. Bundles of euros originally stolen by RHC22 from a Manchester bureau de change. They'd never had a chance to dispose of it before they in turn were robbed of it by the Moss Side Mafia. About €2.5 million, we think.'

I feigned amazement. 'Incredible.'

It really was. The bag had contained much more money. Almost twice as much.

The reason I knew was because I had it.

Chapter Twenty-Eight

The truth, the whole truth and nothing but the truth. That's what you are asked to swear to, isn't it?

The best lies, as they say, contain a lot of truth. Mine certainly did. Of course, it's not the amount of verifiable fact, but the significance of the falsehoods or omissions which define the honesty of an account of a series of events. Nevertheless, a consistent, well-drawn picture of a crime, told by someone who was clearly a victim of it as well as a witness, may be hard to disbelieve. It's about the teller as much as the tale.

By this point in the interviews, the police had already established I was a liar, and a consummate one at that. That skill surprised them, and me too. They uncovered a first layer of lies, but not the others, because my fallback story was as consistent as the original. I found I was able to keep track of the different versions of my tale of what happened, even under repeated questioning. The police are practical individuals. When to finally believe a witness, in the absence of evidence or corroboration, in the end comes down to gut instinct, and much of that is informed by motive. Establish an incentive for the lies, and they are explained. Eventually, Sampson and Coughlan seemed satisfied that they had a reason for my uncharacteristic dishonesty. They believed I had lied about my involvement with Sparko Sinclair purely to conceal my guilt about leading the killers to his home. And that certainly was a major explanation for it. It was a truth which they could read on my face. I couldn't have hid that, if I had wanted to. But as you have now discovered, it wasn't the only inspiration.

I mean, there was an awful lot of cash.

Money was never really a motivation for me, and I never knew from Sparko or anyone else quite how much there was until I discovered it for myself. I don't expect you to believe me if you don't want to. I only ask this: what would you do?

I had recovered all the money, all €4.8 million of it, within ten days of the end of the siege. I knew the exact amount because I counted every one of those 48 thick bricks of euro notes before packing them at the bottom of a giant box of Ethan's Pampers for safekeeping. Then I burned the sports bag and the drugs in a bonfire in my back garden.

So my question to the police, about recovering the loot, was simply to find out how much the police knew, and how successfully I had covered my tracks.

Very, as it turned out.

Chapter Twenty-Nine

Geoff

Here's my wife Catherine, yesterday evening. Tuesday. It's October, two years and three months since my death. I have learned a great deal posthumously about the talents and skills of my beautiful widow. You can see her here, kneeling in the back seat of our, or rather her, new car. It's a rather swish Audi, top of the range. But she is still the same risk-averse Catherine. She is still there with a screwdriver, checking the booster seat for our now three-year-old son. They are off on holiday to the continent, the third visit to Montpellier. As she has now bought a flat there, I'm not sure if they will ever be coming back. She still worries, just like she always used to, but it is just that she worries about different things. After what she has been through, every day is a gift. She no longer worries so much about her moles, though she is still very careful to use sunscreen and to apply it to Ethan, who shares her milky skin.

As Catherine finishes with the screwdriver, she pulls forward the cloth and plastic lining of the booster seat, away from the supporting shell. From my old briefcase she takes a wad of euro notes, and secretes them inside the seat. Only a few of the bundles will fit here, but that's okay. The bulk of them are in the spare wheel compartment in the boot. Having €4.8 million in cash is quite a responsibility. It dwarfs the £100,000 advance she got from my book, our story, which she so carefully tweaked to back up her own version of events. But she is careful to only spend like someone with a hundred grand. She doesn't want to attract attention, even now.

My love for her is undiminished by what I now know. She did what she had to do. She was courageous, smart, and for the most part did the right thing. Her involvement with Sparko Sinclair was noble, generous, and for the most part selfless. In the end, as she told the police, she made the only decision that any mother could. To protect her son. Our son. She had never told me about Sparko, or her first, youthful pregnancy. But sometimes lies, when told with the right motives, are the least of problems. I would just now like to show you the last two pieces of the jigsaw, which will make sense of everything else.

Many of the words are the same, but there are subtle differences. See if you can spot them. And this time, finally you will know that it is true. Believe me. Because I really am dead. And the dead, let me assure you, can see everything.

On that fateful Wednesday, after I had parked the car outside the deli, and gone in with a huge list of Kurdish ingredients and delicacies I wanted to buy, she told me she was popping into the newsagents next door. She didn't of course. We were running late, but it wasn't yet quite ten to four. She still had a few minutes. She had kept the phone switched off all afternoon until then. It was only partly because of the hospital, although that was a decent excuse. She did it because she half expected a nervous Sparko to start ringing her, and she didn't want to have to explain those calls to me. But the moment I went into the deli, she left Ethan in the car seat, locked the car, and promised him she'd be back in two minutes.

The front door to the flats on Walton Road opened easily. There was the smell of rubbish, stale cooking and something else unpleasant that she didn't want to think about. There was indeed a sizeable pile of post on the floor, that would take minutes to go through. Something inside her was urging her to be quick. To just scoop it all up, and go through it somewhere else. Anything that wasn't Sparko's she could drop back through the door later, even another day. But she did turn the phone on, and it rang immediately.

Before she could even speak, he was on to her, almost rude: 'What's been keeping yer?'

'I'm sorry. I told you I had other errands. The post…'

'Forget the fucking post. There's something else I forgot. Go upstairs to the top floor…'

'But I thought your flat was the ground floor.'

'Aye, that's right. That's why it's clever. Now shut up and listen, I don't have time to say this twice. On the left-hand wall of the top-floor corridor is the fuse box for the house.'

'Okay, hang on.' She ran up the stairs two at a time, her footsteps clattering. She reached the second floor, breathlessly and felt for the light switch. A strip light flashed, buzzed then flickered on. The windowless corridor led to two front doors, painted municipal green. The first cupboard she found on the left was a wooden one. She described it to him. 'No, that's just the stopcock to the hot water tank. It's painted grey, come on lassie. Quick. It's only a couple of feet on.'

Then she spotted it. She had somehow expected it to be at waist height, but it was 18 inches high and 12 wide, built into the skirting board close to the flat's front door. She crouched down, and fumbled for the small key on the ring that he said would fit it. Inevitably it was the last one she tried. Inside was an ancient rat's nest of electrics, brown fag packet-sized fuses, looping cables in different gauges and colours, and a large and more recent label with the local authority's logo warning about the danger of electrocution.

She heard a key in the outside door downstairs. The irritable voices of a woman and a young child carried up to her, then a slam. She crept back and peered down into the stairwell. The woman was berating the girl for something. Having parked a pushchair, she began to ascend the stairs to the first floor, with the youngster in her arms.

Catherine returned to her task. 'She's back,' she whispered.

'Then hurry the fuck up,' Sparko said.

'It's all electrics. I might get a shock.'

'Not if you listen to what I say,' he retorted angrily. 'I'm a British Army-trained electrician. Flick the big Bakelite switch on the right up, that will cut the power.' She didn't know what Bakelite was, but she flipped the biggest switch. The building was plunged into darkness.

'Oi. What are you doing up there?' called the woman. Her voice was coarse and antagonistic.

Catherine ignored her, to listen to Sparko, who said: 'Reach behind the circuit board. There's a key taped to it. That's the key I need.'

'It's dark,' she hissed. She flicked the phone's light on. 'Now hang on while I put you on speaker.' As she hunted for the button, she heard the woman downstairs talking to someone. Not the child, the tone wasn't right. She too was on the phone.

'Okay, Sparko,' Catherine said, holding the phone into the fuse box. 'I can see better now.'

'Don't use my fucking name, you moronic cow,' he bellowed, a voice that carried into the corridor. 'Now stick your hand down the back of the board on which the fuses are mounted.'

Furious with him, Catherine did so, and immediately felt a piece of insulation tape, the embossed outline of something metal beneath. She pulled it off, and felt a key come with it. She cut the call to Sparko, turned the phone off and stuffed it and the key in her pocket.

Her eyes had now adjusted to the gloom, which was only relieved by a dim emergency exit sign. She'd heard the tired slap of ascending feet and now saw that the woman was standing at the top of the concrete stairs, just a few yards away from her, on the second floor. Lorraine Caldwell was a sizeable figure in the light of her phone, a toddler in her other arm.

'Tell Sparko they're on their way for him,' she smirked. 'And for you.' She held out her phone as if to take a picture of Catherine. That could not be allowed. Catherine slapped the phone away, knocking it from the woman's hand, sending the only light cascading down the stairwell until it shattered on the tiles two floors below. 'You fucking cow,' she yelled, as Catherine tried to push past her.

But in the near darkness they collided on the narrow stairs and Catherine's full weight fell against Lorraine and the child, who both fell backwards. Lorraine's hand squealed as it slid and then lost grip on the metal handrail, the child falling from her grasp. Catherine managed to grab the banister to break her own fall, but Lorraine and the girl tumbled an entire flight. The child screamed, and there was the sickening impact of something hard cracking on the steps. The child's hysteria intensified, but there was no further sound from Lorraine.

Catherine knew she just had to get out of there, before any neighbours came out. She dared not put the light back on, because then what had just happened would become an incontrovertible reality, with responsibilities and blame and consequences. And Catherine didn't want responsibilities, blame or consequences. She had come in here just to pick up the post. So long as it was still dark she could pretend what she had heard had never happened. That it was some horrible nightmare from which she would wake up without blame. She just came in to pick up the post.

She eased her way downstairs, the light grey concrete leading to the woman's spread-eagled shadow at the first floor landing, her lower legs still resting on the staircase to the second floor. She picked her way across, hesitated at the screaming child, and after a brief attempt at trying to shush her, padded down the final flight. Then she let herself out of the front door into another world, of busy traffic, of noise, of normality.

The thoughts spun in her head: It was an accident. It was an accident, and no one was to blame. The woman was probably just unconscious. No one was to blame. She just came in to pick up the post. That's what she had to remember.

As she walked briskly back to our car, she saw two rough-looking characters hurry past her to the entrance to the flats. It was her first glimpse of Fretwell and Cousins. She reached the car. She had been gone just five minutes. Ethan was looking around anxiously, and started to cry when he saw her. She knelt in the back and hugged him. She looked at the key. It was not a padlock key, as she had told the police. It was actually a grubby car key with a tag of sticky insulation tape. There was no remote-locking fob. She pocketed it, then turned the phone on, wondering where I was. It rang immediately. She didn't give Sparko a chance to speak. 'Yes, I've got it. I'll call you later.' She then cut the line, and switched it off, furious with herself for what had happened. There would be time to give Sparko a piece of her mind later on, but right now she had to get away. As soon as I got back.

'Come on Geoff,' she said out loud, hoping that I would be nearly done. After resettling Ethan she had barely time to think about what to do. First she considered banging the horn to summon me from the shop, but realised that might attract other attention. She looked to see if there was a vacant parking spot further from the flats but within sight of the deli, but she couldn't see one. She was still in the back of the car when she glanced in the rear-view mirror.

In just a few seconds Fretwell and Cousins had jumped in, snatched the car keys from her, and demanded Sparko's flat keys. When she gave them up, they then demanded the key she had just found. With the gun pointing at Ethan, she surrendered it immediately. Fretwell then insisted she call Sinclair to ask him where to bring the key. From then on, it was pretty much the same version that she told the police, apart from the moment when Fretwell, fresh back from murdering Sparko, dropped the incriminating phone down a drain.

Chapter Thirty

I still haven't told you how Catherine came to get the money. That's the very last piece of the jigsaw. Let's go back to the final moments of the siege. The police have just torn open the van doors. Fretwell and Cousins are dead, cut down by police bullets, while Catherine is trapped under Fretwell's body. Ethan is the first to be rescued, plucked from the van by an armed policeman and passed to green-uniformed paramedics who are emerging from an ambulance a few yards away.

Catherine only hears his heartfelt cries.

'Ethan!' she wails. 'I want Ethan.'

'He's just here,' she hears a woman say from a few yards away. 'He's fine. He is absolutely fine.' Two male paramedics gently ease Catherine onto a stretcher, the knife handle still protruding from her leg. They carry her across to the welcoming open doors of the ambulance, towards the piercing anguished bawling of her son. A female paramedic has Ethan in her arms. 'Look,' she says. 'There's your brave mummy. What a courageous mum, eh? Now you just stay calm while we treat this leg for her.'

Soon the paramedic places the child in Catherine's arms. 'Shhh, Ethan,' she says. 'Everything is going to be all right now.'

Safe at last, my lovely wife bursts into tears. With Ethan now beyond harm, she is thinking about me. No one in the ambulance is able to tell her my condition, and she fears the worst. 'Please,' she asks the woman, 'can you ring the hospital and try to find out for me?'

It is only once the ambulance departs for Manchester Royal Infirmary that the paramedic manages to get through on her radio to someone, and is able to relay the news that I am in intensive care.

'Alive then? They would have said if he was dead, wouldn't they?' Catherine pleads. 'You don't leave dead people in intensive care, do you?' She is clutching at straws, and the wan smile from the paramedic confirms it.

'They couldn't give me any details, I'm sorry.' The paramedic then seems to remember something, and fishes an object out of her tunic pocket. 'Is this yours?' It is a car key and a torn tag of insulation tape, now stuck to a dirty scrap of fleecy material. She turns it over, and sees an embroidered rabbit ear.

'Oh, God, it's a bit of Lugs. Isn't it Ethan?' Catherine looked down at her son, who begins to reach for this fragment of his favourite soft toy.

The paramedic laughs. 'He had it in his mouth when we pulled him out of the van. It's dirty and a bit of a choking hazard, especially with a key attached, so I had to take it off him. He wasn't happy about it. Your key, I take it?'

Catherine takes a deep breath, and lies. 'Yes. Thank you. It must have fallen out of my pocket.' In fact it was Fretwell's pocket it had fallen out of, during the fight. From that moment on my clever wife begins to glimpse the possibilities. What a curious thing for this elusive item, Sparko's key, to find its way back to her. And for it to be Ethan, innocent Ethan, who is the agent of this opportunity. One thing is clear to her, even in the ambulance: the finding of the key can never be mentioned to the police. In her first statement she makes no mention of keys at all. That is simple. She doesn't admit to going into the flats, so the issue doesn't arise. But on the third interview, after her enduring connection to Sparko Sinclair is uncovered, she admits the existence of a key. Having done so, she needs a final piece of misdirection to ensure that the police are looking for the wrong type of key.

So when re-interviewed by Sampson and Coughlan, she lies about what she overheard Fretwell saying, as he returned from killing Sparko. She tells the police that he'd said to Cousins: 'It's the key to a lock-up garage. Got the address, with a bit of persuading.' What he'd actually said was: 'It's for a car in a multi-storey. Got the number plate, with a bit of persuading.'

Fretwell's decision to go to that particular multi-storey car park wasn't, as Catherine had said in her police statement, about her abductors hiding away from police. They were there because Sparko Sinclair, while being tortured, had told Fretwell that was where the car was parked, with the sports bag in its boot. It had been moved there a week earlier. After getting the early warning visit that Fretwell was soon coming for his money, Sparko had used his last 50 pence to buy enough fuel to move the car from the lock-up, which Fretwell might know about, into an anonymous multi-storey. The ruse might have worked had not Lorraine Caldwell, seeing Catherine retrieving the key, tipped off Fretwell by phone.

Sparko's bad luck should have made it easy for Fretwell and Cousins. After all, they had found they key and, through Catherine, found him. Fretwell then extracted from Sparko the make and registration number of the car. All they had to do then was to drive there in the anonymous Transit van without the police catching them first.

But in a last act of defiance, knowing he was going to be killed, Sparko laid a final false trail for his tormentor. He had told Fretwell that the vehicle was a green Volkswagen Passat, and had made up a bogus registration number. When Fretwell and Cousins had driven into the multi-storey it was to find this car. But the VW didn't exist. They started at the top floor, and wound their way down. They were only halfway down the seven split levels checking, when they saw the first police vehicle block off the entrance. The lowest two floors would now be impossible to check without running into the cops. The vague plan they had hatched, to seize the loot and scarper, needed to be changed. Only the last word survived. Scarper. But by then the exits were covered by police, and the siege began in earnest.

Catherine wasn't told exactly what Sparko had revealed to Fretwell. But she guessed her captors were looking for a particular vehicle in the car park, and had put two and two together. Five days after the end of the siege, as soon she was able to walk with crutches, DCI Sampson had suggested he show her around the car park, to aid her recollection for her statement. They spent 45 minutes there, much of the time on the floor where the van had been parked. She even re-enacted her role as the gangsters' go-between for food and vodka. On that slow meander, Sampson was good enough to point out where his most prominently placed marksman had been. 'Under that car,' he said, pointing to the Skoda Fabia on the half floor overlooking where the Transit had been parked. 'The car park only reopened two days ago, after CSI had finished. We're just waiting for all the owners to come and collect their vehicles.'

She looked at the Skoda and asked: 'Did you really manage to get a policeman under there? It's a tiny space.'

'A tiny policewoman actually,' he said. 'A damn fine shot she is, too.'

Catherine looked at the registration number, and realised with a jolt that it was familiar. But she didn't say anything. As she walked past, she noted the disabled parking permit, and glanced at the rear window and saw a Motability sticker. That's when she knew for certain. She'd spent enough time working on Sparko's appeal letter, fighting to retain his right to the vehicle, to recognise the licence plate and the sticker. That's when she realised that Sparko hadn't sold the car at all. He had simply put it somewhere for safekeeping.

Ten days after the siege, on a Saturday when the car park

was busy with shoppers, Catherine drove a hire car into the multi-storey, and parked close to the Skoda. It was the work of a minute to unlock the car, remove the sports bag and stow it in the rental vehicle.

Then she calmly drove home. After all she'd been through, she reckoned she had earned it. It would be quite a tale to tell Ethan, when he grew up. How her clever little boy had made them both rich. How he grasped a shiny car key in the aftermath of the siege, almost as if he knew it was important.

Epilogue

So, at last, we come to the final day of my wanderings upon this earth. My beloved wife Catherine sits in a side chapel at Montpellier cathedral, praying, something she almost never did in our marriage. She has Ethan in her arms, and walks up to the statue of the Virgin Mary. Guilt still heavy upon her, she looks to the face of the saint and breathes a brief prayer. She then takes a taper and rests it in the guttering flame of one of the votive candles until a thin curl of smoke begins to rise. She lights three fresh candles to those who died because of her actions on that fateful day two years ago. One to Lorraine Caldwell, one to Sparko Sinclair, and one, of course, to me. It is the last thing I ever see. With a final whisper of undying love, I am gone.

Acknowledgements

I am indebted to Dr Amy Grubb for her expertise in police negotiating strategies and tactics, and to retired detective inspector Kim Booth for his knowledge and experience of police procedure. For the purposes of the plot I have taken certain liberties with the geography of inner-city Manchester, and specifically the service roads and layout of the otherwise real-life Asda supermarket at Hulme. My own 11 years as a Citizens Advice Bureau volunteer helped flesh out Sparko Sinclair's travails with benefits and disability. There is considerable research these days on locked-in syndrome, but for the most engrossing and moving insight I recommend Jean-Dominique Bauby's extraordinary memoir The Diving Bell and the Butterfly. I am indebted to Mark Napier for sharing his experiences as a paramedic, and to Kate Mitchell for sharing her own in the probation service. I thank Dr Jenny Ward and Tim Cary for reading through the manuscript. Any mistakes remaining are my own. The production team at Canelo were right behind this unusual project from the outset, and I thank

Michael Bhaskar and his team for their energy and enthusiasm. To my wife, Louise, always my first reader, go my thanks and my love.

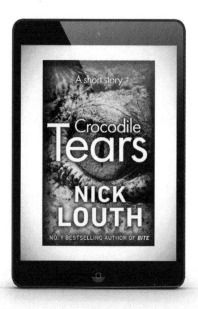